THE Torn PRINCE

zee monodee

First Published in Great Britain in 2021 by
LOVE AFRICA PRESS
103 Reaver House, 12 East Street, Epsom KT17 1HX
www.loveafricapress.com

LOVE AFRICA
PRESS
African Love Stories

ROYAL HOUSE OF SAENE

THE PRINCESSES:
His Defiant Princess by Nana Prah
His Inherited Princess by Empi Baryeh
His Captive Princess by Kiru Taye

THE PRINCES:
The Torn Prince by Zee Monodee
The Resolute Prince by Nana Prah
The Tainted Prince by Kiru Taye
The Illegitimate Prince by Empi Baryeh
The Future King by Kiru Taye

BLURB

Prince Zediah 'Zed' Saene is the sensitive and solemn kind. Nothing shakes him from his solid rock persona. Until the day he crosses paths with Rio, a woman who inflames his body, scorches his heart, and burns his soul to cinders. His passionate love for her is strong enough to move mountains. Then tragedy strikes back home, and he is forced to exit her life without a goodbye.

Riona 'Rio' Mittal has worked hard to get over the contemplative young man who caught her very being in his web of quiet force and soulful presence then dropped her like a smelly old sock. On the verge of setting her life to rights, in walks Zed again to claim the child he's found out she had in his absence.

Zediah wants his heir, and nothing will stop him. Except, 'nothing' has a name: Rio Mittal, who won't shy away from making him face up to his innermost demons. Rio has his son, and all of Zed belongs to her ... yet he is, first and foremost, part of the Royal House of Saene. Torn between duty and love, how will he reconcile the two?

CHAPTER ONE

"AUGUST WOULD be much better for the ceremony, don't you think?"

Zediah Akiina Saene, prince of Bagumi and currently third-in-line for the throne, sighed and closed his eyes briefly as the woman's voice trailed off on the phone. They were now in November, and this was the second time she had postponed their wedding preparations.

Not that he minded—the sigh had been more of relief than anything else. Neither he nor Bilkiss, his betrothed, wanted to get married. He would just about recognise her in a room full of women, her tall stature flirting with six feet the only thing to make her stand out to him. He would bet she'd also have trouble singling him out in a packed crowd.

But duty bade they marry. Bilkiss was the daughter of General Noda, the president of the neighbouring nation of Barakat.

With this alliance, Barakat would be able to stave off the crushing, almost-foregone result of having to replace its bio-diverse rainforest with oil palm plantations for much-needed income. Bagumi's aid and money would help them stay afloat without the need for an ecological disaster.

They would also settle the tiff between Bagumi fishermen and their Barakat counterparts, who always menacingly claimed the neighbours intruded into their territorial waters.

"Zed?"

He snapped out of his thoughts and shook his head. "As you wish."

Again, truth be told, this situation suited him just fine. Aside from this ongoing dispute over their sea rights ownership, both countries were relatively at peace with one another and cooperating.

If they could keep things on this even keel for however long it would last, he'd go along with the fact that Bilkiss seemed in no rush to tie the noose around his neck. Guess she hadn't fallen prey to all the hype about the 'ridiculously handsome and eligible princes of Bagumi.'

How utterly refreshing. On any given day, his brothers would be swatting gold-diggers away as one would pesky flies. He'd escaped a similar fate mostly by hiding his identity during his time abroad, and he hardly made any ripples back here. Not when he had six siblings to take care of that for him.

"Thanks, Zed. You don't know what this means to me," she said.

An echo of his own relief rang in her tone, and he smiled softly. "I want you to be happy, Bilkiss."

She was a nice girl, all things considered. Just not his type, because his type was—

He slammed the lid down on the thought before the train could leave the station.

"You, too, Zed."

He nodded and cut the call. Strange how it still felt a bit odd to hear himself being addressed as such. Aside from his siblings, the people at the palace very rarely shortened his name. When he'd been living in England, he'd had a whole other moniker, a nickname given to him by his friends.

He sighed and threw a look at the expertly appointed suite he called his bedroom. Gilt and velvet, which often felt like the stuffy trappings of a privileged life, choked him regularly, or worse, sucked all the air out of the space, making him suffocate. He'd felt this way almost every time he'd been back at the royal palace in his homeland. Here, princely duties meant no fun, no escape like making music in peace—how unprincely of him to be a 'DJ.'

Technically, he was a music producer, but being behind a mixing console, well, it's what DJs did, right? He shook his head. *Bagumi, Bagumi.*

Though he loved his family, the royal palace no longer felt like home half the time. London did. London, where he'd built a life, one of his choosing, not the one thrust on him from birth.

He needed music to live like people needed air to breathe. Making music helped to balance his life, a sort of self-care. Without it, he was choking.

He closed his eyes. Mistake number one, as all his senses jumped to high alert. Rushing blood thumped against his temples loudly.

Mistake number two was focusing on anything except the pounding pulse. He noticed his tongue growing thicker, blocking his buccal cavity, obliterating the path to his throat.

Arms flailing, he trudged to the French windows and threw the panes open, hurling his body outside into the fresh air. The thick, muggy air proved less than refreshing, with the rainy season drawing to its close this month. Still, it felt less stale than the stifling interior.

Forcing his jaw to unlock, he wiggled his tongue around as he gulped in huge inhales. When the burn in his lungs started to ease, he clasped the wrought-iron railing of the balustrade and let the cool of the metal flow into him. Eyes closed, he paused and focused on his breath. In for four, hold for seven, out for eight.

Minutes passed where he concentrated on bringing himself to a calm state again.

Zediah cleared his head and tried to focus. These episodes had been coming much too frequently lately. True, he hadn't spent this long at the family home since he'd turned eighteen, almost a decade ago. Usually, he'd find a way to split his time between Darusa, the capital of Bagumi, where the royal family lived, and London, with stints in LA and Ibiza or even Hong Kong. But he'd been here for a while, going on eighteen months. This place and its creativity silence was getting to him.

Male laughter and hollers resounded from the ground a few storeys below.

Zediah peered over the railing and groaned, gripping the metal even tighter.

Of course, his brothers would be out there, getting sweaty and buff and becoming even more prince-like. Who on Earth discussed military strategy while doing pull-ups or tossing a ball around?

And, of course, it looked like they all belonged together, all big and sweaty and buff and prince-like.

He had never looked like he fit in. While no one would call him scrawny, it was like lining up David Beckham or Cristiano Ronaldo against a wall of rugby fullbacks. It just didn't add up, did it?

Worse, he'd never *felt* like he fit in with them. Perfect example? Military strategy.

Growing up, he'd been teased relentlessly how the talks around tea and other artistic collaborations he championed were for princesses, not princes. Men got behind diplomatic tables hard and fast, full stop.

As such, he always got pushed into the corner where

he felt like he had to measure up. There'd been a lot of it growing up, testosterone overload and masculine posturing. Although his teen brothers had compared their bicep sizes rather than the length of their dicks, thank goodness! Not that it had stopped them from teasing him when they could.

Zawadi and Zik knew when to drop the ball and cut him some slack. But Zareb?

Zediah groaned. Half the time, he wanted to grab a fencing blade to skewer his Olympic medallist twin. Or get his hands on the pole stuck up Zareb's arse and whack him over the head with it. They were fraternal twins. He would've been seriously perplexed had they been identical, and Zareb had turned out such a stickler for rules and propriety.

Azikiwe—also known as Zik—and Zediah had been the closest when growing up. Two peas in the same pod who riffed on musical instruments during many an afternoon, him on the piano, Zik on his guitar. They'd even entertained the family on numerous evenings.

But what had been okay when they'd been kids and teens wasn't for adults.

When Zediah had left for university, the bond between him and Zik had severed. He'd returned home to find his elder brother had moved on to partying hard with a whole new set of friends Zediah had never really gotten on with.

The ringing phone back in the room intruded upon his thoughts. He released the railing, wincing as the blood returned to his fingers and set off a million pins and needles in them. His digits still felt like sausages by the time he picked the device.

"What's up, mate?" he greeted his best friend, Nick, who lived in London.

"Check your screen," Nick replied. At the same time, a little beep announced a file had come through.

Zediah pulled the phone away to open the picture. His breath lodged in his throat. No, he would *not* let his heartbeat accelerate again.

"What the fuck, man?" he bit out.

"It's the gal you were head over heels for, innit?"

Why on Earth would his best mate rub salt on his wounds?

A realisation slid in then. Salt still made the wound sting because the damn injury was still open. It—his heart, him, whatever—hadn't healed yet.

"Gary *Dick*nell's wife—"

"*Ex*-wife," he corrected.

"Yeah, but you had the hots for her when she was still married to him."

Not something he was proud of, but it was what it was. "And your point would be?"

"You did shag her last time you were here, eh? It was *her*."

"I didn't—" They hadn't shagged. They'd made love. Seriously. Although it'd been the one night, it hadn't been just another fuck for him, and likely not for her, too. But this was Nick, renowned divorce barrister. One never sought to give the man a bone to devour. "Never mind. Yeah."

"Roughly about …"

He sighed. "Eighteen months ago."

More like seventeen months, three weeks, four days, and about eight hours, give or take.

Another ping came from the phone.

"Put me on speaker," Nick asked.

Zediah did as told, then opened the file, and the bottom dropped from everything he'd ever known. His heart started racing again, the thickness returning to his mouth.

Deep breath in. Deep breath out.

The picture was the same as the one that had come

in earlier. Except, it had been strongly zoomed in on the woman before. The complete picture showed her walking in a red coat, pushing a pram, a seated baby clearly visible in it.

A baby with darker skin than hers and a thatch of soft black curls on its head.

While no one would describe her as fair, she wasn't exactly dark, her skin the rich golden hue of roasted peanuts.

But this kid?

"Could be your baby, right?" Nick asked.

The sound of his voice shattered the spell around Zediah, but only just. He could hardly do anything beyond staring at this child. He found himself pinching the screen to blow up the image, obliterating *her* from the frame, his focus only on the baby.

He couldn't be sure, the pixels so grainy at this depth, but if someone had mixed his dark skin with her golden tone, it could come out as this deep toffee little chubby ball. And the hair ... She'd always had stick-straight locks, but the curls here—could the combination with his kinky African hair have resulted in this?

"Switz? Hello?"

He blinked upon hearing the nickname anyone in London or his close friends knew him by.

"When ... when was this shot taken?" he asked.

"This morning. I spotted her on Sloane Street, near the shops."

Zediah frowned. What would she be doing there? Window-shopping, maybe? A stroll out in the nicer neighbourhoods? Her usual destinations were all on Oxford Street, if he recalled properly. Plus, she'd mentioned she was moving back to Southall in West London, where her family lived.

He'd tried to put her out of his mind, had done his darnedest best in that regard. But this? This changed

11

everything.

"How did I not know?" he asked softly.

"She keeps her life very private," Nick replied. "Plus, the paps have moved on to more scandalous WAGs. After her divorce from *Dick*nell, she became old news."

He shook his head. Even when she'd been a WAG— a wife and girlfriend of a famous sportsperson—she'd been more the low-profile type. It only made sense she'd retire into the shadows once the spotlight of Gary Bicknell's numerous extra-marital affairs stopped shining on her.

"She didn't tell me, Nick."

Silence came from the other side. Then, "What are you going to do?"

Zediah took a deep breath and pinched the bridge of his nose. It wouldn't do to act in a rash manner, but if this were his child … He had to find out.

In his heart, he already knew. He'd always thought men spouted utter BS when they waxed lyrical and poetic about seeing their offspring for the first time and their worlds shifting, but he'd been a total idiot. Because he, too, knew. This child—a boy? Girl? —was his. And there was no way as a father he wouldn't have a place in its life.

"I'm coming to London," he said.

"Crash at mine," Nick said. "I'll be in Singapore for the next two weeks."

"When are you leaving?"

"Already on my way to City Airport. I'll see you when I see you, mate."

"Okay, sure."

He would've loved to have Nick there with him, but this was something he had to do. Alone.

Now, to get to London.

A knock on the door interrupted his musings.

The man in the hallway bowed. "Her Majesty Queen Zulekha has requested you join her, Your Highness. She is in the Winter Garden."

As he groaned inside, Zediah, however, acknowledged the servant and nodded. He would've done it by name, but these men and women in livery seemed to go through a revolving door, making it hard to keep up. This irked him—he'd always prided himself on his human touch. The world of music had no place for evident class distinctions, and he carried this viewpoint with him everywhere.

The man turned on his heel and shuffled away, leaving him standing on the threshold as he contemplated whether he could get out of this summons. Fat chance, though. His mother would be waiting, expecting him to get there yesterday.

Then there was this matter of needing to leave for London. He hadn't stepped foot outside the country since his return. As they all loved to remind him, he'd dropped his bombshell, which had had its terrible consequences. Never would he live it down, and he'd taken the edict to stay put and finally behave in a princely manner as penance for what he'd done.

He could nip to London quickly and be back right away with his child, couldn't he? His parents wouldn't begrudge him that, surely. Best not to let them know about the baby, though. Under no light would it look good for a royal prince to have fathered a child out of wedlock, let alone not know of the kid's existence even close to a year later. He already had enough ticks in the 'Black Sheep' category as things stood.

With leaden feet, he trudged from the second floor of one wing to the ground level on the other side of the royal compound, where the prettier gardens were located.

A burst of cool moisture touched his skin as he

entered the conservatory known as the Winter Garden. Orchids bloomed inside this structure, reminiscent of Changi Airport in Singapore. Consequently, the temperatures were kept to a low twenty-three degrees Celsius year-round. When the mercury flirted with forty and above, this place earned its name fully and proved to be a welcoming abode in the scorch of summer.

Until one spotted the occupants—usually either Queen Zulekha or Queen Sapphire, the king's two wives. And just Zediah's luck today as both women were at the glass-topped wrought-iron table sipping tea like, well, queens.

He paused a few feet away to give a deep bow in respect, then straightened when his mother issued the words for him to rise. Going to the table—and resisting the urge to sigh, or run, or both—he bent to drop a soft kiss on Queen Zulekha's taut, walnut-brown skin.

"Mum," he greeted his birth mother.

Then he moved to the other side of the table to place a similar kiss on the smooth, cinnamon-rich cheek of the king's second wife. "Mama Sapphire."

"Sit down, dear boy," Queen Sapphire bade. "Will you have some scones? There's the Devon clotted cream you love so much. Freshly arrived just this morning."

They knew his weakness, and it was pointless fighting any of these women. And when they were both in the same room? Absolutely futile to protest. So, he sat down and reached for a scone, slicing it, and loading it with thick clotted cream and the gooey strawberry preserve made by the palace chef.

He had just taken a bite and was savouring the treat when the first salvo landed.

"So, what has Bilkiss said?" his mother asked.

The piece of scone in his mouth turned to dust. Well, not really, but all the delightful tastes just evaporated to be replaced by this sickening and unpalatable dryness of plaster. He knew what that tasted like courtesy of Zareb punching him right through a plaster-lined wall being renovated in the east wing when they'd been teens. Zediah had made his twin eat dirt in retaliation.

But back to the here and now.

Zediah forcefully chewed and tried to swallow, taking a big gulp of hot tea, and hoping it would wash away the sludge on his taste buds. The liquid burned the roof of his mouth, but it didn't matter.

"What do you mean?" he managed to throw out.

Queen Zulekha waved a delicate hand in the air. "You were just on the phone with her."

And she knew this how? He shook his head. Didn't matter; she knew, aka the end of it.

"Is she ready to talk to the wedding planner? We were thinking a February wedding, what with Valentine's Day and all," his mother continued.

"We could even schedule it for February fourteen," Queen Sapphire quipped.

This was going too far, way too fast. Again, the later that train decided to leave the station, the better. For him, and for Bilkiss, it seemed.

"So, what does she think?"

He focused on his mother and made sure to hide his wince. "She was thinking more along the lines of August."

Both queens blinked.

"She wants a wedding in the next dry season?" Queen Zulekha asked.

"But it's ages away," the other woman supplied.

He just shrugged. "Well, it is *her* wedding."

"And yours," his parent pointed out.

He gulped. He really did *not* want to think of it. Maybe they could come to a compromise, he and Bilkiss. A marriage of convenience, in name only. He wouldn't

15

have any issue living like a monk. He had for the past eighteen months. After her—

He stopped himself right there. He would *not* think of her. Not here. Not now. Not in this scenario.

Because if he did, he would remember how she was the only woman who could make his blood boil, shake his lust from the dormant state. In his late teens, he'd worried, wondered why he just didn't seem to be drawn to any woman. He'd even questioned if he could be attracted to other genders. But it had been the same kind of cold spell there, too.

Until he'd seen *her* for the first time.

"Zediah, I imagined you would be taking this more seriously," his mother said. "What would your father …"

The cunning queen left the words unsaid, something which stung him even more than if she'd actually said them. Oh, she knew how to play the guilt card. In fact, his whole family knew how to pull that one on him after what he'd done following his return from London.

And speaking of London …

"Mum, I need to be away for a few days."

Queen Zulekha frowned. "Whatever for? Did your brothers ask this of you? I didn't know we needed to send an envoy to visit an ally."

And again, what she didn't say was what smarted the most. Ally. They usually sent someone like him—inexperienced in politics and military strategy, and with 'useless' knowledge about music and its world—like a clown to a nation where he wouldn't rock the boat in any way.

To any place not an ally, he just wouldn't cut it, would probably put his foot in his mouth. Embarrass them at best and jeopardise world peace at worst.

They just didn't 'get' him, did they? Frustration roared inside him, firing up his blood. They'd taken his music from him, chosen a wife for him—did they also need his dignity?

"I need to head back to London," he stated calmly.

This calm control was one of his fortes—not that *they*'d know—how he could appear unfazed and unruffled outside while a storm, often a shitstorm, raged in him.

"Whatever for?" his mother bit out with a disapproving frown. "I thought you'd put all this nonsense behind you, Zediah." She shook her head. "We really shouldn't have been so lenient with you. I see it now."

His eyes narrowed as he stared at her. But a soft nudge from a shoe against his foot under the table bade him to calm down. Of course, Mama Sapphire was there to smooth ruffled feathers. *She*'d always come through for him—he shouldn't forget it. And Isha, his half-sister.

"How long?" Queen Sapphire asked.

"A few days," he replied. "A week, at most."

His mother sighed. "If it's to put your past to rest …"

"It is," he confirmed.

She sighed. "Fine. Do let Zawadi know first, will you?"

And just like that, his temper boiled over. He didn't need a keeper, and he certainly did *not* need to have all his movements recorded by the Crown Prince and the stickler-for-rules known as Zareb.

"Mum, just once …" He bit his tongue on the rest. First, one did not speak like so to their parent. Second, especially not to a queen.

The teacup clattered so hard in its saucer, he feared the fragile china wouldn't make it in one piece.

"Music, Zediah? Is music so important to you? You've had your fun. Don't forget you're betrothed now!"

And on and on it would go in a similar vein—he'd heard the same chorus before, carried loudly by his mother, his father, and his brothers.

"I have a child!" he burst out.

A stunned silence descended on the Winter Garden. Both women were staring at him with wide eyes and open mouths.

Queen Sapphire blinked first. "Who ...?"

Damn it, he'd let the cat out of the bag now. No way could he retract. Yet, it *was* true he was going to London to retrieve his baby. Why did he have to hide this from his family? They would be this kid's family, too.

He gulped back and shrugged. "A woman I got involved with briefly before I left England."

No one important ... Though who was he kidding but himself with the thought?

"She has a child?" Mama Sapphire continued. "And it's yours?"

He shrugged again. "I believe so, yes. Though I'm not sure yet."

Officially, that is. His *everything* already knew.

"My first grandchild," his mother whispered so softly, he thought he'd imagined it.

"Indeed," Queen Sapphire concurred.

But more than the words, it was the awe in them that gripped his heart in a vise and refused to let go. His two mums would love this child to bits. His sisters would spoil the kid rotten. And the king ... His father might finally be proud of him, even though he'd not gone about the proper way to bring a baby into their world.

"Is it a boy or a girl?" his mother asked softly again. Gone was the bristly political strategist, replaced by a doting grandmother in the blink of an eye.

"I don't know yet," he admitted.

She nodded. "You'll bring him or her home?"

His turn to nod. "Yes, Mum."

Because this was where his child belonged, with its family. Not to tout his own horn, but he *was* a royal prince, which did have its perks sometimes. His child would grow in a palace, with the best upbringing money could afford, a chance to see the world, to *be* someone.

Rio ... For the first time in seventeen months, three weeks, four days, and give-or-take nine hours, he allowed himself to recall her name. Riona. His Rio.

She would want the best for her child, wouldn't she?

Now to make her see he was the best thing for their baby, for all the opportunities he could grant the kid, which she probably couldn't. He would never fail to acknowledge she had a mother's love for their son or daughter. Surely, she, too, would come to see Zediah could give their baby the finest future one could afford in today's world.

CHAPTER TWO

RIONA 'RIO' Mittal sighed as the phone rang yet again that Sunday. Her mother, of course.

Maybe she could ignore it for just this afternoon. With a tug, she pulled the front door of her Clabon Mews freehold house in Knightsbridge so it would close with a soft thump. Next, she slammed her other foot on the brake of the pram and stopped it in the entryway.

Coat off and scarf unwound, she then divested her son of the many extra layers on him before picking the baby up and placing him on her hip.

Why did it seem to be getting much colder so soon this year? She'd never had to be in many clothes in November. But things just seemed to come in way faster nowadays.

Case in point, all the Christmas decorations that had already made their shiny and blinking appearance. All they needed was Mariah Carey to start blaring from the speakers inside the department stores. Come the actual Christmas, everyone would be sick and tired of the music and screaming in their heads to have it turned off.

In her arms, the baby gurgled, then burped, the accompanying spit-up drooling all over her shoulder. A groan escaped her. Thank goodness she'd already removed her cashmere coat. The thermal top could go in the laundry, like the entire collection that made it through the delicate cycle every three days, it seemed.

"Nour, baby," she cooed to her son. "Can we please stop with the spit-ups? Pretty please, sweetheart?"

Nour just watched her with his big doe eyes, then threw his head back and laughed.

Okay, so he would not cooperate. What had she expected? He was a mini-bloke already. She sighed. But she loved him to bits, though, and he had her heart—she would thus probably forgive him just about anything.

Yet, by the same criterion, someone else had owned her heart once—no, twice—yet she hadn't forgiven them, had she?

Shaking her head, she forced herself to leave those dodgy thoughts behind and focus on her main reason for living now, aka her son.

Rio shuffled farther into the house, her socked feet sliding on the wood floors in the main reception space making up the best part of the open-plan ground floor, on her way to the stairs at the far end. She paused near the kitchen island as a blond head emerged from the staircase leading to the lower ground level and basement.

"You're still here?" she asked Oksana, her live-in nanny. "I thought you had a date today."

The pretty Russian girl smiled and shrugged. "Not for another hour. I just need to hop on the Piccadilly line, and I'll be there in a few minutes."

Rio nodded. "And who is it this time? The environmental protection start-up bloke, right?"

Oksana shook her head and laughed softly. "You keep better track of my dates than I do!"

"Living vicariously through you, love. So, I got it right?"

"Yep."

She frowned at the young woman. "You don't sound too convinced."

Oksana shrugged again. "I don't know. I just keep going to dates that are absolute busts every time."

Nour started fidgeting in her arms, and she switched him to the other hip, where he promptly ducked his head into her neck and started gnawing on her hair. Oksana quickly reached over and pulled Rio's long locks to her other shoulder where the baby wouldn't be able to get them.

Rio started bouncing the child to stave off a teary episode. Nour did not like having his toy of the moment taken from him.

"It's only your ... eighth date, innit?" she asked.

"Feels more like eight-hundredth," the blonde replied with a sigh.

Rio chuckled. "Come on. He could be 'the one' this time."

Her phone rang again, the Bollywood ringtone assigned to her mother.

Oksana frowned. "It's your mum."

"I know." She huffed.

"If you need to go see her, I can take care of Nour here."

Rio narrowed her eyes at her. "No, you don't. Sunday is your one day off, and you have a date. Plus, you're ..."

She was going to say, 'you're all decked out,' but it was apparent Oksana hadn't tried. Though she didn't need to, to be honest. Who needed to make an effort when they were twenty-three, and the world was at their feet? Though less than a decade older, Rio had long lost those rose-coloured glasses. And she needed to make an effort daily.

Not really rejoicing. Her spirits sank. The ringtone cut, only to pick up four seconds later as the song started back again. Great. She would have to answer this and then pander to whatever puerile request her mother would be sure to voice out from the western end of London in Southall.

Oksana was already reaching for Nour, but Rio swerved in the opposite direction. She would not take the chance of the nanny getting vomit on her pretty Topshop dress and then bail out of her electronically arranged date.

"Off you go," she intoned.

Oksana groaned but gave her a smile and dropped a kiss on Nour's cheek. The baby took the opportunity to lunge forward, his mouth coming into close contact with his mother's hair that he promptly started to chew on again.

Rio winced at the pain when chubby fists wrapped into the locks to tug hard. Still grimacing, she followed Oksana to the entrance hallway, making sure the girl put on her coat and scarf.

"Don't forget gloves."

Oksana rolled her eyes. "I'm from Russia, Rio. This is almost spring weather for us."

Did this mean, given how both her parents were originally from hotter lands—her father from India, her mother from Mauritius—she had become averse to the slightest hint of cold?

"Still," she muttered. "And be nice! Give him a chance this time. He could be—"

"*The one.* I know." This earned her an eye roll.

"Okay, shoo."

She smiled as the younger woman left the house and started in the direction of the Knightsbridge underground station. Closing the door, she hopped back inside, just as her phone started ringing again.

"Yes, Ma," she answered.

"*Ene bonzour nanié pa gagné ar toi aster!*"

"Good morning, Ma."

She sighed. She should've seen the reprimand

coming—her mother was a stickler for propriety, which implied a suitable greeting every time. Another sigh tried to escape. Her mother had used Creole, and that bade nothing good. There went her quiet afternoon putting Nour down for a nap and then catching up with whatever Villanelle was up to in the latest season of *Killing Eve*.

Thankfully, her mother switched to her heavily-accented English, which sounded like a French person trying to pass for British, but failing miserably yet having no clue.

"There's a problem with the seating plan."

Rio groaned softly inside. Of course, there would be.

She was essentially a millionaire now, thanks to the divorce. So, whatever it was, they would need her to swoop in with her chequebook and smooth it all out with a few hundred—or thousand—pounds.

"What happened?" she asked, taking the stairs up to the first floor where the nursery was located. Baby balanced on her left hip and phone cradled to her right ear with her shoulder, she'd pay for the contortion later.

Her feet left the Turkish runner on the staircase to plunge into the soft carpet on the first-floor landing. She reached the playmat in the corner of the largest bedroom, lowered the baby, and retrieved the phone in her grip. Yep, her neck was killing her already.

"You have to come, Rio *beti*."

Okay, so not only did her mother sound hysterical, but she'd also buttered her up with this little endearment that meant 'darling daughter' in Hindi.

There would be no way out. Not with her mother. Never with her. Best she buckled up and met it all head-on like she always did.

"Give me one hour."

Sighing, she cut the call, relieved and slightly worried her mother had not protested at all and urged her to get there quicker. Whatever brewed must be significant.

Sixty minutes would give her just enough time to take a shower, change, and feed Nour a snack as it would take a little more than half an hour to get from Knightsbridge to Southall by car.

Indeed, an hour later, she parked her Range Rover Evoque in front of her family's restaurant in Southall.

Her grandfather, who'd arrived here in the early 1950s, had nabbed a property right on The Broadway, which had ended up becoming the main thoroughfare and foodie street of the area.

Exiting the vehicle, she averted her gaze, avoiding the blinding glare of sunlight on the chunky gold necklaces displayed in the window of the Indian jewellery store next door. Walking to the other side, she grabbed Nour from his car seat.

No point bothering with a stroller here as there would be half a dozen pair of arms, at least, to take the baby from her the minute she stepped foot inside.

With a few long strides to cross the pavement, which always struck her as extra-wide, she strolled into the dimly lit interior of *The Jolly Maharajah*. 'The Jolly Rajah' had already been taken by another family who'd opened their eatery a few streets down. Yet, her family had considered it their good fortune that the other place had gone bust a couple of years later.

"*Sat Sri Akal*," she greeted as she passed through towards the back and met the mostly Sikh workforce of the restaurant. A few '*Namaste*' made their way in, as well as a single "*Assalam Aleikum*" to the lone Muslim employee—a Pakistani chef—in the kitchen. They opened for dinner on Sundays, only from five o'clock onwards, hence the deserted front eatery at this time of the afternoon.

Holding the baby tight, she started up the steep

staircase leading to the family home in the two storeys above the ground floor.

"*Roshan beta*! Come to *Nanima*!"

Her mother descended upon them in a flurry of colourful dupatta—the wide fabric scarf she always wore as a shawl draped over her bosom—and the clink-clink of thick gold bangles at her wrists.

"Hello to you, too, Ma," Rio mumbled, knowing it was pointless.

Pointless to ask to be seen. Pointless to mention, yet again, that her son's name was Nour and not Roshan, though both names meant the same thing, 'bright light,' the former in Urdu and Arabic, the latter in Hindi. Trust her mother to make such distinction obvious.

Nour tried to scramble away from his *Nani*'s arms, and Rio could clearly see a bout of crying making its way up. Thankfully, in strolled her father, and Nour slung his whole weight towards his *Nanaji* and gurgled happily.

The kid really seemed to dislike the too-effusive faffing that, frankly, rang terribly false and overdone. He must have sensed the hypocrisy the older woman wielded so well yet seemingly unconsciously.

Her mother pretended she adored the child whenever in his presence. Yet, she would never fail to let her daughter know she'd clearly have preferred a much whiter grandson. Or that Rio should count herself lucky she hadn't had a daughter instead. Implying the girl's fate would have been sealed almost like that of an Untouchable back on the Indian sub-continent circa the Partition era.

"Namaste, Papa," Rio greeted her dad. She smiled as he dropped a soft kiss on the side of her head and gave her a gentle one-armed hug while holding her son to his other shoulder.

Nour wasted no time plunging onto her dad's

hanging spectacles and started to chew the chain dangling around his neck. She quickly retrieved him and fished for a teething ring from her bag, stopping the waterworks just in time.

Sounds came from the staircase on the far side of the room, leading to the second floor where her brother Rajiv and his wife Minnie lived. Her sister-in-law was all smiles as she came down and made a beeline for the baby, who happily lurched in her direction to be swept up in a massive hug and cuddle.

Rio shook her head. Funny how Nour hated to be held like a baby by her or Oksana but seemed to revel in it when in his *Mamee*'s arms. Perfect—she could now leave her son in capable hands and attend to the matter that had brought her here.

Or not.

Her mother stood before a seated Minnie and Nour with a wad of money in her grip. Her hand moved in concentric clockwise circles in front of the girl's face, then switched direction as the cadence of the prayer changed, too.

Next, Hema Mittal wailed and threw her arms up to the sky, begging God to make the child here a conduit of its blessing to finally place a baby in her daughter-in-law's womb.

And here we go again.

Poor Minnie's fair skin turned pink with embarrassment. She'd been married less than two years, for God's sake. But of course, she should have already popped out a child—preferably a son for her first-born—nine or, at most, ten months after her wedding night. With her alabaster complexion and crow-black hair, Minnie was considered the ultimate beauty, the perfect bride. Now, if she could only be the perfect broodmare, too.

"Here." Her mother waved the wad of money she'd

used to remove the evil eye on her daughter-in-law and thrust it into her husband's hand. "Go give this to Hamid. He could sure use it."

Rio's mouth dropped open, as did Minnie's across the room.

"Ma! Don't you pay him enough as the cook? He won't take charity, for sure," she blurted out.

Her mother tsk-ed. "Those people are always looking for handouts, aren't they?"

Rio shook her head with disbelief. When would the woman realise she lived in England now and not Mauritius? How culture and society matters were different here. Just because someone was a Muslim, like their Pakistani chef, didn't mean they were asking for charity. Even if most people who went house-to-house seeking alms on the tropical island happened to be mainly Muslim women.

Her father softly shook his head and went downstairs. Flabbergasted, Rio watched him leave. She always thought her mother couldn't shock her more, but she was proven wrong almost every time she set foot back here.

Thanks to all the rocking and cuddling, Nour appeared to have fallen asleep.

Minnie stood up. "I'll put him to bed upstairs."

Rio nodded. "Please, thanks."

The other woman made a hasty retreat upstairs, away from her mother-in-law's scathing tongue. Rio couldn't begrudge her, though. If she could run, she would, too.

Her father came back up, and he pulled his hand slightly out of his trouser pocket, giving her a hint of the turquoise bundle of five-pound notes his wife had stuffed in his grip earlier. He gave her a soft wink, then retreated to the study at the back of the house where he could escape his wife.

Rio stifled a smile. She couldn't fault him for running away.

Turning, she trudged into the kitchen, where her mum would thrust the inevitable cup of chai at anyone who set foot inside the house.

Since her pregnancy, milk added to strong tea made Rio nauseous. Yet, her mother never took note of her aversion or chose to ignore it. Fine, she could nurse a cuppa for the two hours—hopefully, just one hour—she'd be forced to endure here.

So, she plopped down at the Formica-topped kitchen table and wrapped her hands around the mug, welcoming the warmth despite the central heating docked at twenty-something degrees Celsius on this floor. One could never get enough heat in a British winter.

Her mother parked herself down across from her, extending a plate of *jalebis* her way. She shook her head. Another collateral damage of her pregnancy—she couldn't stand the smell of the grease they used to fry those funnel cakes in before dunking them in thick syrup. Again, her parent hadn't noticed.

The plate landed with a thud on the table. Hema Mittal took a deep breath, then closed her eyes and brought her hands up to press her temples.

Rio's stomach lurched. *Uh-oh.*

"You will not believe what that *girl* has done," her mother spat out as she opened her eyes and stared at her all agog.

She didn't miss the extra-spit and hiss on the word *girl*. Of course, they'd be talking about Tanya, her youngest brother Rishabh's fiancée.

"What happened?" she asked, more to be polite than anything else.

"She invited the whole Ismail clan to the reception!"

29

Okay, the Ismails were a big family. Grandparents, three sons and their wives, if she weren't mistaken, and between them, they must have about a dozen children. Still, it didn't warrant this kind of panic. They were planning an Indian wedding—until the last minute, they *would* find themselves shoving tables to make room for uninvited guests and even wedding crashers.

"We can always add more tables," she voiced out.

"But what about the food?" her mother shrieked.

Rio frowned. "What about it?"

"Well, they'll want Halal, won't they?"

"And?" She didn't see what the problem was.

"Well, we don't do Halal, do we? Vegetarian, yes. But they'll be expecting their *kofta kababs* and *chicken tikkas*, and the *goat biryani*, of course."

Rio had to force herself to remain calm and stay in her seat. The proper thing to do would be to fight her mother to include Halal meat slaughtered as per Muslim rites in their kitchen. Bam, problem solved. Not like it would be hard for them to find Halal meat in Southall, or even London nowadays, for that matter.

"Do you wish to seat them at the vegetarian tables?" One couldn't expect devout Muslims to eat meat not slaughtered in the way their religion demanded. Still, they could eat anything meat-free without any issue.

Her mother gasped, her hand landing flat on her heaving bosom as her eyes grew even bigger in her round face. "And lose face in front of everyone? That girl, I tell you ..."

Anyone listening to her would think Tanya to be the devil's very own offspring. But her only 'fault' was that she was dark-skinned—*walnut baklava* to Rio's less-dark *toasted coconut* if one were to use foundation shades to compare them.

And where it hurt her mother most was, her

precious Rishabh had been born with flawless fair skin. As such, the boy was expected to marry a girl even paler than Minnie—as if it were possible—and not this dusky chit he'd fallen in love with who would surely give him muddy-skinned babies. Oh, the shame and horror ... *That girl* must have hexed him into falling for her, too.

Footsteps rumbled on the staircase leading to the first floor, and a few seconds later, Rishabh and Tanya appeared in the front room.

Her mother got up from the kitchen table and all but floated to greet the young couple.

"Rishabh *beta*!" She embraced him as if she hadn't seen him in six months, not just six hours since he'd left the house in the morning, most probably. "Tanya, *beti*."

And *that girl* got the same treatment, along with a saccharine tone and over-effusive hugs. No one would think the older woman had just been word-bashing her with her daughter barely two minutes earlier.

Rio didn't bother to join them yet—the prancing of the mother goose in there would render any movement impossible in the tiny room. So she took the opportunity to dunk her undrunk tea in the sink and waited there with her hip propped against the wood-topped counter.

The other three people converged into the kitchen, turning the cramped space into the equivalent of a fish-in-oil tin.

"Hey, sis," Rishabh greeted.

She smiled as he kissed her cheeks.

Tanya came all in for a hug—she'd been expecting it, having figured out the girl operated on only two levels: enthusiastic and over-enthusiastic. Still, she made Rishabh happy, and it was what mattered. Nothing but happiness and love.

A pang hit her heart when she reckoned how, twice, she'd thought this kind of future lay ahead of her. What a dummy she'd been.

"Rio, have you seen this?" Tanya tugged her towards the screen of her phone, which displayed a picture of some wedding party. "Isn't this the bloke who's terribly smitten with you?"

She hardly had a minute to peer at the image before her mother snatched it from Tanya's hand.

"Oh, look, it's darling Megha's wedding. I didn't know they'd released the pictures," she cooed.

Rio grimaced softly and exchanged a loaded glance with her brother.

'Darling Megha' was Megha Saran, someone they didn't know from Eve or Saraswati and Lakshmi and Parvati. But the young woman from Surrey was of Indian origin, which almost made her family.

Plus, in their circles, the fact Megha had snatched one of the most eligible bachelors of Europe, Magnus Trammell—not to mention a White billionaire—put her in the first spot as *the* example to follow and the goal to aspire to.

"Oh, yes, it *is* the pasty-faced boy who's always at your functions, Riona," the older woman continued, squinting at the screen then turning the phone towards her.

Rio bit her lip when she made out the face of Humphrey Prentiss standing next to the groom. As the ninth Earl of Bodenlea and Trammell's family friend, he would have been invited to the exclusive party.

"But he's a bit gay, isn't he?" her mother continued, then shook her head. "Never mind. You can change him when you're married."

Both Rio and Tanya now had their mouths hanging open, staring aghast at the older woman.

"Ma, you can't say things like that," Rishabh finally blurted out.

Hema Mittal shrugged and rolled her eyes. "What, it's true."

32

"No, it's not," her brother continued. "If someone is one way, you can't change them."

"Ha! As if that's the case. A generation of pussies is what it all is now. He's sweet on you, Riona. Use what God gave you since you're so intent on it already and get yourself this man as a husband. You already let a good one go."

Stunned silence descended on the room.

Rio didn't know which one in this tangled yarn of insults she should focus on first. Her mother would never let her forget she'd gotten pregnant out of wedlock and hadn't born a white man's child.

At worst, the older woman hoped Nour's father was a darker Indian man. God forbid, he was a Black man, especially one of those West Indies or Jamaican types!

Rio had never enlightened her.

And as for Gary.

No one knew what her life had been like with him. He hadn't cheated at first, and he'd never hit her. Didn't meant he hadn't been abusive. Why would he need to use hands, fists, or kicks when his words had always landed the blow harder than blunt force could? Then the infidelities had happened, followed by him demeaning her at every opportunity inside the closed confines of their house, especially their bedroom.

No one knew. No one except ...

Unable to stand the recriminations, Rio rushed out. She stumbled down the flight of stairs, escaping via the service door into the cold air tinged with reeks of rubbish from the bins a few paces down the alley. Bent double, hands on her knees, she let the blood flow back into her head and forced herself to breathe from her mouth.

As her heart rate refused to calm down, she finally paused to acknowledge it. The dig about Gary hadn't hurt. Not really. Not when she knew what she'd escaped from when she'd walked out on him.

No, it had been something else. Something she hadn't wanted to look at, let alone contemplate. For all the days since she had woken up in the bed of the guest bedroom of her St Johns Wood house to find it empty, any trace of him gone. Fine, she'd thought—she could, and would, put him behind her.

Then two weeks later, her regular-as-clockwork period had been late, and she'd known. She was pregnant, and she hadn't even known the actual name of the man who'd fathered her child. Switz Bagumi, it turned out, was a stage name. No one seemed to know the identity of the man who had simply disappeared off the face of the Earth after spending a night of red-hot passion with her.

Switz ... She had pushed to forget him, to ignore the very thought of him.

Thank goodness Nour hadn't taken after him much, and she thus didn't have to look at his likeness every day. He had waltzed into her life—three times!—and left her reeling every single time. If that didn't highlight the score where she and men were concerned, she didn't know what would.

God, she always sucked with the opposite gender, didn't she? Or even at life. Here she was, over thirty, a single parent, with a bigot for a mother, and absolutely no prospects.

At this, she blinked. The last one wasn't technically true. Humphrey was indeed sweet on her; if she were to give him any hint she'd reciprocate if he made a move, he would be hers. And such a kind, sweet person, too, would be hers in body, heart, and soul. The body part, she didn't much care for, not with him, not after—

Do not *think of Switz!*

But the heart and soul ... If only she could belong with someone ... Just once ...

Would it be too much to ask?

Standing in that stinking back alley, Rio took a deep breath to fortify her resolve and stood up straight. She could still get her life together and make something of her future. For her and Nour.

Tomorrow, at work, she would speak with Humphrey and tell him she was open to him courting her.

CHAPTER THREE

AFTER SNEAKING in a kiss and cuddle from Nour on Monday morning, Rio escaped back upstairs to the master bedroom suite she occupied on the second floor of her house.

Oksana would feed the baby his porridge downstairs in the kitchen. A feat which implied all surfaces around the kitchen island and the highchair would be covered in dribbles of baby food. Thank goodness for easily cleanable treated wood floors.

In her bedroom, she flopped on the edge of the bed, grabbed her phone from the nightstand, and called Kelsey Clegg, her boss who had somehow morphed into her best friend over the past year. The call connected, Kelsey's sultry voice answering on the second ring.

"I need your help," Rio said, not beating around the bush. Neither of them was a fan of such behaviour.

"Hmm ... What can I do for you?"

Deep breath—*here goes*. She wouldn't be able to backtrack after this.

"The gala on Friday. Is Humphrey attending?"

"Humphrey Prentiss? No. As far as I know, he declined to attend in his RSVP."

Hope swelled in her chest. That was good; it meant he hadn't been snapped up by another woman.

"Any reason why?" she asked.

"Said he didn't like to come to these things alone."

Better and better! "Think he'd agree to come if I asked him?"

A few seconds of silence stretched from the other end.

"He'd jump off Tower Bridge if you were to ask him." Kelsey huffed. "You're really gonna do this?"

She knew what the woman meant. Kelsey had seen her in her direst hour after the divorce and then Switz's desertion, which had brought her to her knees even more than leaving Gary. The two of them hadn't made a pact or anything of the like, but she had a feeling they'd both committed to living their lives for themselves after having had their hearts trampled.

But the question really begged her to consider her reply. And she did.

"I don't love him, Kel. I'm not *in love* with him. But I can be good for him."

"He's a good man," Kelsey concurred.

"He is."

"Call him. Ask him to be yours."

Her friend didn't just mean for the gala— Humphrey seemed to be in for forever, it seemed.

Precisely the kind of solace and security she needed for hers and Nour's future. Humphrey already adored the baby, and he wasn't the kind of man who would tell her to leave her kid behind with her family to be with him.

"Thanks, Kel," she muttered. "We should meet up to debrief later."

A sigh came from the other end. "No can do. I'm only flying back on Thursday night."

She frowned. "Where are you this time?"

"Shetland. They're shooting the scenes for the first episode of season three."

"Oh, the pain of your life," she quipped with irony.

Kelsey Clegg was a nationwide literary phenomenon whose best-selling series of crime books had been made into a hit TV show. As its executive producer, she had to be at many filming locations, especially those crucial to the story.

"Ha! Text me later. Let me know how it goes."

"Will do."

"And Rio? Make an effort, will you?"

"Very funny. See you Friday at the gala."

With this, she cut the call, a smile on her face. She should be making an effort today, indeed. Though Humphrey had seen her at her most harried, with her minimal makeup having long disappeared, and despite him seeming to not have a problem with that, she owed him more.

So, for today, she decided she'd deck herself out in a cashmere jumpsuit as she'd be mostly at her desk all day long. She also took special care with her makeup, adding a flick more mascara to open her eyes. She switched from lip balm to the rosy-berry hue of her lipstick, which always worked so well to bring out the olive undertones in her complexion under their best light.

After sliding on a pair of pointy toe-ed ankle boots, she went down the stairs to the study on the first floor, where she grabbed her laptop bag, then sailed down to the ground floor. She paused on the edge of the reception room, viewing the kitchen with a dubious twist of her lips.

The island did indeed look like a porridge bomb had gone off, and Nour was laughing away as Oksana tried to feed him the little still there in the bowl.

The baby gurgled and waved at her, a plastic spoon clutched in one chubby fist. Perfect—he was in a good mood. She could get away with blowing him a kiss and shouting she loved him all the way to the front door. Not as fulfilling as a hug, for sure, but cashmere just did not do well with puree splatters, and she was a woman on a mission today.

The roads were a bit of a pain this morning—and it would only get worse the closer they got to Christmas—and it took her over thirty minutes to reach the building she called work near Camden Market. Located near renowned nightclubs and artist galleries, Tempo was an NGO giving youngsters access to dance programs and a safe day care environment where they could just be themselves and have fun.

Rio was its Executive Director, reporting to a board of directors which had Kelsey as its chairperson. She'd never thought she'd move to administration. She was first and foremost a yoga and dance teacher who'd joined the staff as an instructor.

She'd figured out the windfall she'd received in the divorce would only take them a decade forward if she wanted the best education for her son. So, moving to this admin position had seemed like a godsend.

She parked the Range Rover in the tiny side garage provided for the building and hopped her way to the front door. This early in the day, the youths who frequented the place wouldn't yet have arrived to turn the interior into a thumping bass dance floor. Thank goodness for soundproof walls, which had cost them a fortune but had been so worth it. The vinyl shop next door had tolerated them before. Still, things were less frosty with the owner and the clientele now.

Her staff, consisting of a few dance instructors, greeted her from the floor. Her assistant, Martha, got up when she strolled in. A large-size travel cup of steaming black coffee already in hand, Martha followed Rio into the office and placed the drink on the table.

The woman rattled off the many tasks on the docket for the day.

Wincing, Rio reached for the coffee and took a big

glug so the caffeine would enable her to keep up with Martha.

The first time she'd heard her assistant's name, she'd expected a dowdy granny type.

Instead, she'd met a bubbly blonde in her thirties who should've been named Tiffany or Annabelle or some other such effervescent name belonging to a preppy cheerleader.

Rio rearranged the piles of files on her desk, trying to find the accounts folder she needed to review for the day. A knock on the still-open office door made her look up.

A tall, gangly-limbed blond man stood there.

"Humphrey," Martha said with a wide smile. "We weren't expecting you today."

Rio slanted her a quick glance before rising from her seat to greet him with a kiss on each cheek. "I was just about to call you."

He smiled. "Guess fate already knew, then, since I had this insane urge to drop by."

As one of their biggest benefactors, it wasn't strange for him to pop in every so often. Though she would admit, he had been here a bit more in the recent months. Could this be a good sign for her?

"Cuppa?" Martha asked him.

"Wouldn't say no," he replied.

The other woman left the room.

"Sit, please." Rio waved at the chair opposite the desk, knocking over a pile of folders in the process.

He grabbed the papers before they could hit the linoleum floor.

She reached for the files at the same time, and his hand landed on hers.

It was warm, soft, and very smooth. Of course, as an aristocrat, he'd hardly ever put in a day's work, and not the manual type. Aside from these sensations,

40

nothing rocked her, not even slightly, let alone to her core. Raising her eyes, she glanced at his face.

His kind smile obliterated that he looked more like the frog than the Prince Charming in the eponymous reference. Especially with his bulging grey eyes and broad shoulders not at all in proportion to his long, stick-thin legs.

He had a good heart, though, and this she knew from having seen him so many times trying to help the kids who came to Tempo for a brighter chance at life.

Files safely back on their pile, Rio and Humphrey sat down.

Martha returned with the tea, placing it on the table. With a big smile, she left and closed the door behind her.

Rio took a deep breath and bade her time as he took a sip of his tea. Best not to beat around the bush. She wasn't a simpering miss by any length, and she wouldn't turn into one today.

"So," she started. "About the foundation's gala this Friday ..."

He put his cup down and faced her. "You're going, of course. I doubt Kelsey would let you off the hook."

She laughed softly at this—Kelsey could indeed be scary when she wanted to. Now to take the plunge. Deep breath in. "I was hoping you could be my plus one."

He blinked for a second or two or three. "Are you ...?"

"Asking you out on a date? Yes."

Well, that had come out easier than she'd thought. Guess she'd just needed to wade in.

He blinked again, then his big smile overtook his pale face. "Sure."

A pang hit her heart. He seemed happy. While she wasn't toying with him, she should let him know what it all boiled down to. Deception was one of the hardest

41

things to get over and to forgive—something she didn't want between them.

"Humphrey ... I'm not in love with you."

There, she'd said it. If he told her to go take a flying leap, then so be it. She would not con someone into believing they had a bright future with her to then pull the rug under their feet.

He remained silent for a while, studying her, which made her squirm. Yet, she resisted the urge.

Finally, he took a deep, audible breath. "I'm not going to blow up my own person by saying something like 'yet' or whatever. But I suppose you like me?"

"I do," she replied quickly. "A lot."

"Then that's good for me." He reached over, palm upturned.

She reached out, placing her hand in his. Again, gentle warmth seeped into her where they touched.

"I'll be honest, Rio," he said. "I'm not looking for love. Companionship, a nice person by my side. I'm okay with that."

She nodded. "Fine by me, too."

He smiled, then brought her hand over to drop a soft kiss on it. "So Friday's a date, then."

"Sure." As he got up and reached the door, she called out to him. "I won't let you down."

He gave a soft nod. "I know."

When the door closed on him, Rio let out a breath and sagged against her seat. Everything still looked the same around her, but at the same time, it was all so different.

With those last words, she couldn't help but think they'd exchanged a promise to be together. Like a tacit agreement to a proposal which had been hovering in the room, yet not voiced.

She glanced at her left hand, the third finger devoid of a ring for the past two years. There might not be a diamond there, but she could feel it—the engagement.

Going into a marriage of convenience, yes.

Still, she had her eyes wide open this time, and she would honour this man who was giving her a second chance so generously.

Now, work. She had the whole day's agenda to attend to. Plus, it seemed those hooligans they all loved so much had started to arrive, the percussive electronic notes of a Martin Garrix EDM track already thumping in the floor.

Martha strolled in with a folder in hand. "He seems in a good mood."

Rio nodded. "We're going to the foundation gala together."

"Oh."

She glanced up just in time to see the crestfallen expression on Martha's face, which was replaced with a smile a fraction of a second later. For a moment there, Rio wondered if she'd conjured the look, if the grin seemed forced.

She must be imagining things.

She sighed, taking the thick folder, and placing it on the heavy pile of accounts documents already awaiting her on the desk.

"Martha, do not let me out of this office until I give you the budget revisions for the coming year."

"Done. Coffee?"

Rio nodded. "Keep it coming."

Hours later, and after about three large refills of her travel mug—who needed lunch when they powered on caffeine—a knock came at her door.

For once, she'd been able to blip through the youngsters' ruckus. Martha would come in and out soundlessly to top up her coffee. Why, then, would her assistant be knocking?

She paused in her task and looked up, still seeing

numbers blurring before her tired eyes. Great, she'd forgotten to get a new bottle of eye drops. She'd ditched the last one, which had been opened for a month already on Friday.

"Someone here to see you," Martha said through the ajar door.

And without an appointment, indeed. Still, NGOs like this existed thanks to donors and benefactors. It wouldn't do to send any prospective helper packing.

She gave a soft nod and started to get up. The leg of her jumpsuit caught on the wheel of her executive chair. She peered down while trying to dislodge the delicate fabric before it got tangled to an irrecuperable mess.

The air shifted in a strange manner as someone entered the office. A whiff of a light citrusy cologne hit her nostrils. It smelled like ... No, she would *not* go there. There must be so many men who wore Dolce and Gabbana's *Light Blue*.

Pasting a smile on, she looked up, only for the gesture to freeze like a rictus on her face.

There, by the door, stood a tall, lean man in a suit. The dark blue colour deepened his skin's rich chocolate tones, which stretched over taut, chiselled features, and a severe mouth one would think never broke into smiles.

But he had smiled, for her, with her ...

Try as she wanted to shake her head, she couldn't. Her pulse jumped. She'd never thought she'd lay eyes on him again. She certainly wouldn't have expected to do so with him in this kind of attire when he'd favoured jeans and loose linen shirts in the time she had known him.

Where those outfits hadn't been able to hide the almost-feral streak in him, the suit took it to a whole other level. With his close-cropped hair—so different from the playful locs he used to wear in a loose ponytail at his nape—he looked like a billionaire tycoon who should be on the cover of GQ or some other influential magazine. His narrowed eyes highlighted his innate ruthlessness even more.

Those eyes. Dark, almost black, and with a hint of grey-cast quicksilver when the light hit his irises exactly right.

Eyes affixed on her right now, making her squirm, making her yearn, making her burn.

He'd always had this effect on her. Ever since she'd first spotted him, he had stirred her insides and burrowed a place into her heart with every subsequent encounter.

This man who'd loved and cherished her for one night and had left her in the lurch.

"Switz."

The name came out with all the ice she could conjure. Steel infused her being like the adamantium coating the bones of the claw-handed superhero, the rapid beating of her heart slowing somewhat.

"Rio."

The sound of her name flowing from his tongue was like a pleasure-drugged moan, a caress, wiping away her remaining stupefaction.

In a blink, anger flared in its wake, shaking her up, igniting her blood with a different kind of fire—deadly frostbite rather than raging flames.

"What are you doing here?" she bit out.

She forced herself to stand tall and straight, grateful she'd worn the cashmere and lipstick which felt like armour, suddenly, when they'd been merely feel-good earlier. And praised be the heels which allowed her to stare right into the abyss of his dark eyes, without having to tilt her neck back too much.

No way would she allow any emotion, any feeling, *anything*, to come through when she was forced to stare at him less than four feet from her.

The man had almost made her lose herself, had

toppled her world when she'd believed it had already been as topsy-turvy as it could get.

"We need to talk," he said softly.

He'd always had this manner of speaking at such a low pitch where she thought she'd imagined his words, much less heard them.

Crossing her arms in front of her chest, she tipped her chin forward. "About what?"

The expressionless mask on his face didn't move, his eyelids not blinking once. She would almost say he was as frozen as a statue.

"About my child."

The wind got knocked out of her upon hearing this. So he knew ... How?

But he had some gall coming here to say this after the runner he'd done on her. Her eyes narrowed.

"*My* child, Switz. *My* son."

"It's ... a boy?"

She rolled her eyes. "I didn't say 'daughter,' did I?"

"I have a son."

Finally, he blinked, and this incensed her more than anything else in the past few minutes, which was really saying something given how much he'd rocked her to her core.

"You don't."

"Rio ..."

She huffed at the hint of menace in the word. Who did he think he was?

"He's *my* son, Switz. Conceived with your sperm, sure, but he's mine."

He stayed silent for a long second or two. "Means he's also mine."

So that's how he would play it? She hadn't survived—thrived—on her own for the past eighteen months for him to just breeze in here today when the coast was clear to play the righteous prick with her!

46

"He is?" she spat out. "Then where the hell were you when I found out we'd made him? The day he was born? All those sleepless nights and the endless doctor's appointments—"

"Wait, he's sick?"

He'd already taken a step in her direction, and she stopped him with a raised hand. "Check-ups and vaccination schedule."

"Thank God," he sighed, his shoulders deflating a little as he stopped in his tracks, now just three feet from her.

Rio blinked upon seeing this. "Thank God? That's it? And what if he *had* been sick, Switz? What then? What would you have done? Oh, wait, you weren't even here, were you? Makes absolutely no difference for you to waltz in here today like I owe you the world—"

"Rio—"

"I owe you *nothing*, Switz Bagumi! Nothing, you hear?"

"Riona—"

"And don't you 'Riona' me now with that sweet tone!" A bitter laugh escaped her. "You know so well how to play the nice bloke card, don't you?"

"It's not like that—"

On a roll now, she paid only the slightest attention to the larger-than-life presence with which he'd crossed over the threshold. For once, she thanked the kids outside for their love of eardrum-ripping music.

"It's not like what, Switz?"

He closed his eyes for a moment and took a deep breath. She so wanted to sock him one for seeming like he was the one trying to hold on to control.

When he finally looked her way again, the fire in his gaze almost made her want to take a step back. But she didn't. She would stand her ground this time. For her. For Nour.

"You didn't tell me about him, Rio."

Seriously? He thought he could come here and throw this at her?

"I would have ... In fact, I was desperate to tell you."

"Then why didn't you?"

Her eyes almost boggled out of her face then. "*Why*? Tell me something—do you even exist, Switz Bagumi?"

He huffed. "Of course I do. I'm standing right here in front of you."

Hai Rabba. Could any person be this obtuse? Not to mention the fact he'd made her call upon God like a good Bollywood drama queen. Did this incense her more, actually?

"And what's your real name, pray, tell? Coz I sure don't know it!"

"It's Zed," he bit out.

She blinked at this, her mouth dropping open. Well, it was a start, but still ...

"Zed? Like the letter? Who the hell do you think you are? Some major hotshot artist like J Balvin or J-Lo who goes by just using an initial for their first name?"

"It's short for Zediah."

"Now we're getting somewhere. Hi, my name is Riona. At least a proper introduction, finally. Go on. You're Zediah what?"

Did he hesitate for a fraction too long before answering her?

"Zediah Akiina ..."

"Man, I have been so far off from Switz Bagumi in looking for you."

"Rio—"

"Don't you *Rio* me! Don't you dare!"

Did she just get as undignified as projecting spittle when she said that last one? She hoped not. Though dragon flames would've been more than welcome, to burn to cinders this clueless idiot who stood there as if ... wait a second. He seemed to have deflated to a mere man after standing there so mighty all along.

Great. Served him right.

Suddenly, it was as if all her bluster and rage and fire just died, like snuffed out with the snap of one's fingers. What were they doing arguing like kids during recess on the playground?

A sigh escaped her, and she tottered towards her chair before falling onto it with an undignified plop.

"What do you want, Zediah Akiina?"

She no longer had it in her to fight him. As if she'd scorched through the recrimination and festering hurt and anguish she'd carried all this time, cauterising the wound in the process and leaving just a tinge of pain smarting around the edges of her heart.

He still stood there.

She would surely have flung a paper weight at him if he'd had the gall to come sit opposite her when she hadn't invited him to. Guess her anger wasn't so far gone, after all.

"He is my son, too, Rio." He paused. "What ... what's his name?"

"Nour." Saying her baby's name brought a soft balm over her ragged emotions, and she gave a weary smile.

"It means 'bright light'."

She nodded. "Yes."

"I ... I should've been here for him."

For *him*. Not for her. Not *for you* ... She bit her lip to stop the pain from electrifying all of her.

Because nothing else mattered to him. His child. He wouldn't have come back just for her.

What an idiot she'd been to hold on so tightly to the idea in the deepest, darkest reaches of her brain, never mind her heart?

"It's not too late," he went on.

She simply raised an eyebrow in reply, too battered in her soul by now to do much more.

"I can give him a good life, Rio."

"And I can't?"

The words hung between them. He had the decency to look chastised and peer down, anywhere but at her face. There might just be hope for him. Just.

A snort escaped her when she thought back to all this. Never mind how he'd found out about Nour. He was a year and a half too late, and too much water had run under the bridge. She had been giving the best life possible to their son already, and when she'd marry Humphrey, they'd be a family, too ...

Who did he think he was, storming in like this and staking claim now on the child she'd borne, given life to, and cared for during all this time he was AWOL?

"Get lost, Switz. Zed. Whatever your name is." She chuckled without mirth. "Shouldn't be hard for you, given how you already know so well how to do that, don't you? Just leave."

CHAPTER FOUR

ZEDIAH TRUDGED back to Nick's house in the cul-de-sac of Park Place in St James, the return trip happening in a daze. He must have taken a cab there, but he didn't remember. His surroundings only registered when he found himself in the marble-decked lobby of the grand four-storeyed house. With a sigh, he plopped down on the thick sofa flanking the massive curving staircase.

He shook his head. What had he been thinking?

And that was probably it—he *hadn't* been thinking. Guess living in a palace where everyone except his family kowtowed to him had made him soft. Made him forget real people didn't treat princes like royalty when they had no clue who said princes were in the first place. A snort escaped him. Not that Rio would've cut him any slack were she to find out about his royal status.

He'd left when she'd so sneeringly told him to. What else could he have done? He'd instinctively known in his gut, a quiet, subdued Rio was the one version of her no one could ever go against. He could definitely go toe to toe with her when she was all fire and flames and passion. But the cold ice she'd displayed today? Even he knew when he should run for the hills, and he had.

Again, what had he been thinking? Barging into her workplace to confront her and try to make her cower before his mighty status?

Bloody fool. He should've reckoned this would never work with her.

Riona Mittal fought tooth and nail when she believed in something. The woman he'd seen today had embodied this kind of calm certitude and solemn grace. Any straight-thinking man would know bullshit couldn't get past her.

He'd gone to Tempo expecting to find her there. The NGO was her life. He hadn't missed how invested she'd been in those youths and the joy inside her when she danced. He, however, hadn't expected the big office at the back, much less to find her name on the door and 'Executive Director' under it.

So, she'd gotten promoted in the last year or so.

The woman he'd glimpsed in the room upon first entering had struck him as being the epitome of beauty and class. Elegant clothing, skilful makeup that looked like it wasn't there, and smooth dark hair in freshly blown strands brushing her chest and shoulder blades.

Until she'd looked up and met his gaze, and he'd seen the same woman who had robbed him of breath every time he'd lain eyes on her. She still had the same power even now. He'd been struck speechless ... until she'd spoken out his name.

Well, his nickname. She'd never known him as anything else. He'd conveniently forgotten that. How could she have looked for him when she didn't have a clue about his real identity? Looking for the surname Bagumi in the telephone directory of his homeland would be like trying to find someone named Smith in England, otherwise known as a needle in a haystack. Add to it not even knowing the person's first name, and the needle actually disappeared.

Damn it! He'd dropped the ball on this. No wonder she'd been so furious. He'd fucked up. Royally, too! A mirthless chuckle escaped him.

Against his thigh, his phone vibrated again. He'd silenced the device a few times this afternoon, but the fact the calls kept on coming meant someone from his family was trying to contact him. He should stave off the inevitable and respond. Maybe his mother would let him off the hook when she found out her first grandchild was a boy.

Nour.

Just thinking of the name made his chest hurt. When would he get to see his baby? Not anytime soon, while Rio was angry with him. Her parting words ... Of course, she'd think he'd walked away from her without looking back. Which he'd done. Bloody idiot.

Pulling his phone from his trouser pocket, he allowed himself a slight smile when he saw the name 'Isha' on the screen. His sister. Not his mother. He'd take this call gladly.

"Hey, sis," he greeted.

"I can't believe you didn't tell me! How could you, Zed? You are a father! With a child. A *child*!"

He winced as he moved the device away from his ear thanks to her rushed shouting.

"Who told you?" he asked.

"Mum! I can't believe I had to hear this from Mum!"

She meant Mama Sapphire. Of course, his other mother would inform her children. His own mum ... suffice it to say she was a stickler for state secrets and the like. Not one for gossip, even when it pertained to her own bloodline.

A sigh let loose from his lips. "I was going to tell you."

"When? After the apocalypse?"

He snorted. It might be awfully close to the truth, the apocalypse named Mama Bear Rio. He'd really put

53

his foot in his mouth there.

"After I meet him myself," he said with a sigh.

"Wait, what? You haven't even met your son? Daughter?"

"Son. His name is Nour."

"But how come? You've been in London for more than twenty-four hours. I would think you'd get this done. Hold on, is the mother playing hard to get with you? You know she can't do that legally. You have rights—"

"Believe me, she's perfectly in her rights here." Best he stopped his lawyer slash activist sister on her roll before she started building a custody case for him already.

A pause came from the other end. "But he's also your child."

"I know." He took a deep breath, since pointing out the truth did demand a good dose of courage. "But I messed up, Ish. It was my fault."

She remained silent for a long time—so long, he wondered if the call had dropped. This had been known to happen in Wanai, where she lived with her husband. The country was still recovering from decades of a despotic regime.

"Who is she? Tell me about her."

Zediah closed his eyes as he settled more comfortably on the sofa.

"Her name is Rio," he started. "Short for Riona. I met her five years ago ..."

***

Five years ago ...

"Come on, Switz. It will be fun."

Zediah threw a glare at his best mate. "You want us to celebrate graduating our LLM by the skin of our teeth, not through a pub crawl, but at someone else's party?"

"He's a mate. Gary. Just got engaged."

He rolled his eyes. Trust Nikhil 'Nick' Varendra to always have a social diary overflowing with invites. Zed, who'd come to London to study for a degree, had never thought he'd find a friend, much less a kindred spirit here.

But it turned out Nick was also a royal—the third son of an Indian maharajah, born from the king's brief marriage with a White Englishwoman. Nick's older brothers couldn't stand him. The fraternal animosity they shared against their male siblings had bonded them in an unbreakable way.

Yet, it didn't mean he didn't want to throw his boot up the other man's arse at times. Like today.

"Who the fuck is this Gary, anyway?" he asked.

"Gary Bicknell. You must have heard of him. Football player, brilliant mid-field who's said to be the next David Beckham. Plays for Ashton Rovers. Looks like they might be making it all the way into the Premier League next season if things keep up."

He had no care or concern about sports and its celebrities. But he'd tag along since it was Nick asking. And the idea of a pub crawl alone just didn't appeal.

They found themselves, shortly after, in North London. The party was taking place on the official grounds of the football club. They made their way to the VIP floor, where an open bar already overflowed. People mingled amid raucous laughter and a blaring remix of Fat Boy Slim's 'Right Here, Right Now.' Zed huffed. At least the DJ didn't have bad taste.

"Nick! My man!"

He turned to see a tall, dark-haired bloke converging towards them to man-hug Nick. When he pulled away, his pretty face worthy of being the leading man in a boy band broke into a massive smile.

Nick then introduced him to, he'd already guessed

it, Gary Bicknell.

"Millie's around somewhere," he said. "Can't wait for you lads to meet her."

He assumed the Millie in question was the fiancée.

They made their way to the bar where they each got a pint, and he settled back to people-watch as Nick saw someone he knew in the crush and went to say hello. Zediah would give him an hour, tops, before hightailing it out of there.

He was scanning the big room with his eyes when something in the corner near the DJ station caught his attention. A flash of red, moving softly, sinuously, in rhythm to the beat. Something about the sight made him pause and watch more carefully.

It was a woman—a beautiful one. Possibly the prettiest he'd ever seen. She had beautiful golden skin that reminded him of the rich hue of roasted peanuts. Offset by the orange-red shade of her dress which fell to mid-thigh, her complexion positively glowed. The caramel streaks in her shoulder-length, straight dark hair made her face radiate even more.

And what a face, too. Feisty was one word he would use to describe her delicate features, from her button nose to the narrow forehead, pointed chin, and soft cheekbones catching the light exactly right.

He had to blink when he realized he had been staring at her for so long. His eyes had gone dry. No one had ever had this kind of effect on him—he had to meet her, find out who she was. With determined steps, he made his way towards her.

The closer he got, the more she seemed to captivate him. Such as when he saw her mouth up close. She'd swiped a shade of lipstick matching her dress perfectly on her full, pillowy lips that seemed to beg a man to kiss them, to tease the slight pout into opening for him.

And her eyes. Big and bold, dark at first glance, but

actually a lighter brown with pronounced flecks of hazel in the irises. The scent of her up close—something sweet, like candy, yet soft as well, reminiscent of pretty, dainty flowers. Utterly intoxicating ...

As his heart rate accelerated, Zediah knew it already. Love at first sight. No wonder he'd never felt stirred by any other woman in the past. Because none of them had been *her*.

She had a graceful, lithe body that undulated right along with the rhythm of the music. No one would've labelled the track as sensual. But watching her, it dawned on him.

She'd even make a marching band playing off-key sound like music to drive a man wild with desire and longing. And it was all in the way she moved. Lascivious, purposeful, titillating, yet never vulgar. She knew how to tight-rope that fine line so very easily.

He hadn't realized he'd kept on moving, and he bumped into her. Thankfully, she'd just shifted the other way, and the beer sloshed over the back of her hand and not on her dress.

She turned to him then, her gorgeous eyes flicking up to his face before registering the still-full pint in his hand.

"Are you drinking that?" she asked.

She'd spoken to him! Her voice had a soft, gravelly hint to it, the accent sharp and rapid, the kind he'd had trouble keeping up with when he'd first moved to London a few years earlier. It wasn't the clipped, sharp Queen's English he was used to in royal circles but more like a local dialect.

"Are you?" she asked again, eyebrows raised in question, too.

He shook his head, and it seemed to be all the prompt she needed—he watched, his own eyebrows up, as she reached for the glass and downed half of the

Guinness in one long gulp. Smiling, she licked the froth moustache on her upper lip before handing him back the pint.

"Thanks …"

"Pleasure," he mumbled, his brain still stuck on the sight on her pink tongue licking her upper lip.

She frowned softly then gave him a cheeky smile. "Your name is Pleasure?"

At this, he blinked. Damn, he should try to focus here. In no dimension would it help his game to come across as a dimwit.

"No," he scoffed. "Why d'you ask that?"

Strange how they were able to have a conversation without needing to shout. Guess being this close to the DJ's turntables, they were enclosed in a small bubble while the loudspeakers blared all around the room.

The frown let up on her face, leaving just the smile behind. "Well, I said thanks and was waiting for your name, and you said Pleasure."

It's how she should always look: alive, alight, glowing, with a flicker of mischief in her sparkling eyes.

She seemed to be waiting for his reply, though. *Get your game on, man!* Now he'd found her, he couldn't let her go, not through his own faux pas.

"My name is Switz."

By this point, it had become second nature to use the moniker and not his given name. It helped a lot to see people's reactions when they thought he was just a regular bloke and not a prince.

Her eyebrows rose again. "Switz? What sort of name is that?"

He couldn't help it—he chuckled. There'd been just stunned curiosity in her tone, not a dismissal or some hoity-toity sense of being superior. "Short for Switzerland."

"Ah." She tilted her head to the side, the long locks

brushing the exposed collarbone, the neckline of her dress having dropped beyond her shoulder. "So, I assume you're neutral and all."

"Exactly." He smiled at her then, loving her carefree banter and the warm and friendly vibe coming from her. Again, not something a man could interpret as vulgar and a come-on. She just seemed like a genuinely lovely person.

"Switz," she said slowly.

The sound of his nickname flowing from her tongue hit him in all the right places. His trousers grew tight. Damn. He should bring this back to an even keel.

"And you are?" he asked.

"Rio," she said, extending her hand.

"Like Rio de Janeiro?" he asked. The name would suit her, what with her being so bright and larger-than-life even at first glance.

Thank goodness he'd spoken by the time he clasped her hand. The mere touch proved enough to burn to oblivion the remaining functioning brain cells in his head.

Her skin was so warm, so soft, and her long fingers felt fragile and delicate in his grip. He'd never considered himself a big or hefty man. Not compared to his brothers, who had been wearing XL T-shirts since their teens.

But with Rio's hand in his, he suddenly felt like a bloke, a *man's* man. Everything inside urged him to wrap her in his arms, physically and figuratively, to protect and cherish her in his embrace forever. As she deserved, and nothing less.

Her bubbly laughter tore him from his thoughts, as well as the ill-advised urge to crush her to him, demand her mouth and seek permission to worship her body if she'd allow it.

"Just Rio," she said. "Short for Riona. Mittal."

"Mittal?" He'd heard the name somewhere.

"Oh, I see where your mind is going. Not *those* Mittals. We're from dodgy Southall."

It dawned on him then, *those* Mittals being the steel tycoons worth billions. He shrugged—it must be a common enough name for people of Indian origin.

"I wouldn't call Southall dodgy," he ventured to say.

Her eyes grew big. "You've been there? Seriously?"

He nodded. "Loved those little fried cakes they sold on the main street. What are they called—"

"*Jalebis!*" she said with a laugh as she clapped her hands together. "You actually tasted *jalebis!*"

"And liked them." The deep-fried funnel cakes soaked in thick syrup had indeed been delicious. "Maybe I'd like a lot more if you were to show me around someday."

His own bluster astounded him as the words spilled out of his mouth. He'd never had game. Guess it would come into play when necessary, inspired by Rio's presence.

Before she could respond, someone barrelled into her, pulled her close, and dropped a deep kiss on her lips. She pulled away and pushed the bloke with a hand on his chest.

Zediah shifted, ready to punch the disgusting prick who had assaulted her. However, her trilling laugh stopped him in his tracks.

"Mistletoe," Gary Bicknell said with a wide, smart-arse grin as he waved a festive green and red branch over her head.

What the fuck? What was the buffoon doing, kissing random women at his very own engagement party, no less? The poor chit who was marrying him.

"I see you've already met my Millie," Bicknell said as he turned towards Zediah and pulled Rio tightly into his side.

Everything around him froze to black, the light shining only on this couple before him.

Her name was Rio, though, not Millie. What was going on?

How could this be going on?

And he'd looked at her left hand at some point. She hadn't worn any jewellery there.

"I didn't see the ring," he said softly. He hadn't missed it, surely, being so totally obliterated by her.

"I'm a bloody fool, mate," Bicknell said with a laugh. "Got one too big and had to send it back to be resized."

When he dangled the mistletoe again over her head, she laughed and pushed him aside. Nevertheless, probably to soften the blow, she dropped a kiss on her fiancé's cheek and giggled when he grabbed her waist and crushed her to him.

Her fiancé.

The one woman who'd caught his attention in his twenty-three years, and she was taken already.

Darkness slowly crept up on him and shaded his heart which had beat so hard and fast just mere minutes earlier. He couldn't stay there any longer. He would wonder why he hadn't crossed her path earlier before she met Bicknell. Before she found love with another man.

Mumbling an apology as etiquette was something that had been drummed into him from his youngest age, he then turned on his heel and hightailed it out of this party.

***

Three years ago ...

Zediah breathed a sigh of relief as he once again found himself walking along the snow-coated streets of London during the holiday season. He'd turned twenty-five during the year, and it seemed to have been code in his mother's eyes, meaning he was now of marriageable age. Not a week went by when he was back in Bagumi when some matchmaker or another wasn't sending in an illustrious proposal for him.

He didn't kid himself. Born a prince in one of the last absolute monarchies in the world, he would most certainly be marrying for duty and not love, never mind that he was the spare to the actual spare. But he was twenty-five; he hadn't lived enough already.

His older brothers Zawadi and Zik had told him it was par for the course. They, too, had been afflicted by this manic need to see them settled with a noose around their necks asap. He had time, surely.

And just as well, really, because he didn't mind needing to marry for duty and country. The only woman who had ever stirred his heart was happily married to someone else. He would cave only for her. Not going to happen, though.

So, he'd made a pact with himself. He'd marry at thirty to whoever his family deemed fit.

In the meantime, he would keep on spending his time between Bagumi and London. It hadn't been easy to wrangle his way back to the English capital after graduation. His sister, Isha, had sweet-talked Mama Sapphire, who had, in turn, sweet-talked the king. Zediah had been allowed to pursue humanitarian work with aid agency *Angelos* at their headquarters on Canary Wharf.

On the side, he made good use of his specialisation in entertainment law as an angel investor with young music artists who wanted to go indie or who were setting up their own record labels. He'd always been drawn to music, playing the piano as a five-year-old without taking music lessons. The notes just making sense to him as he experimented with the keystrokes.

The keen ear enhanced his work—he almost had the

knack of figuring out who and what the next big thing would be in music, just by listening and trusting his gut.

In this capacity, he found himself walking towards Camden Market, where the NGO Tempo was located. He'd heard about the dance recital they'd organised for the annual Lighthaven Foundation gala to raise funds for its many charitable endeavours.

Unfortunately, Dilmas, an artist he'd invested in, who was supposed to produce the original music for this performance, had gotten embroiled in a legal battle with his record company. It sucked all his time, leaving these kids in the lurch.

But not as long as Zediah was there.

He found the building where the organisation occupied two-thirds of the ground floor, the remaining part holding a vinyl store in its premises. The thump of pounding music already thrummed in his blood as he stopped in front of the door—guess they did not have soundproof walls. Then again, they were an NGO; these never had enough budget for anything, let alone frivolities.

The blare grew louder when he pushed the door open. Across the polished wood floor, he could see his reflection in the mirrors covering the entirety of the far wall.

"And five, six, seven, eight!" a woman was repeating in a lilting cadence as she led the group of young dancers into an elaborate routine that frankly impressed him. He'd seen professional dance troupes put on less rhythmic and flowing choreography.

He stopped to watch them, transfixed. They were good, and so was the teacher. He'd have to find out who had come up with this arrangement using chairs so skilfully as a prop. Though a laudable cause to help out here, that person was seriously underusing their talent.

He had been so caught up in the flow and flips and

kicks all done seamlessly, it took him a few seconds to reckon the song had ended and the performance had stopped. Unbidden, his hands started clapping. The kids all turned his way, as did the teacher.

His hands clapped, then froze. It took just a flash to recognize her. Rio Mittal.

No, Rio *Bicknell*.

So she was a dance teacher? No wonder she had moved so well on the day he'd seen her. The same day he'd known he'd never have anything with the one woman who had caught his heart forever. The organ hadn't beaten for anyone before or since.

She blinked upon seeing him there.

"Switz?"

Something in her tone made him pause to really look at her. She seemed ... different. Fragile. Despondent, even. No longer the shining beacon she had been on the day of her engagement party.

Had something happened to her?

Was that prick not looking after her?

He should cool his heels. She wasn't his, would never be. But something in the way she looked ... really like her light had dimmed, wasn't right. The sensation stopped him in his tracks.

It suddenly dawned on him how everyone was looking at him, so he shook himself out of his unrighteous feelings and gave her a curt nod.

"Rio," he bit out.

She blinked a few times, then smiled at him, and he saw a glimmer of that girl in there, the radiant personality that couldn't help but shine so bright.

"What are you doing here?" she asked.

Business. He was here for business. "Meeting with Ben Scholes."

She nodded. "Ben got caught in traffic. If you're in no rush, you could wait for him in his office. Let me take you there."

"Sure."

He followed her, just a pace behind. At least they had good heating inside this building. He'd fear for her health otherwise because of the thin workout top moulding to every curve of her muscled back. He didn't dare let his gaze wander lower as he'd already ascertained, with a quick glance, how enticing her arse looked in the yoga leggings.

"Here we are," she said as she pushed open the door to the office and waved him in.

"Thanks. So, how are you?" he asked.

They were, essentially, strangers since their first meetup had hardly made them acquaintances. But more so than small talk, he wanted to know how she was doing. As much as he tried to fool himself, he cared for her.

"I'm ... good," she said with a smile that rang fake as it never touched her eyes.

He also didn't like the hesitation in her tone.

"You?" she asked.

"Fine," he bit out.

She nodded softly. "Well, if you'll excuse me?"

"Go."

He settled down in one of the seats, grateful the dance floor wasn't visible from the office once the door closed behind her. But something kept niggling at him, and he yearned to find out.

Zediah had never been one for gossip, but maybe it would help shed light on why Rio's light seemed to have gone out since the last time he had seen her.

Ten minutes later, he powered down his phone while wondering if he could break something while imagining the prick, Gary Bicknell's face, as the object.

Bicknell had indeed made it into the Premier League, making Rio a WAG. Added to his good looks, he'd earned a direct passport into the world of sports gossip. It also appeared Bicknell couldn't keep his dick in his trousers, fucking a new trollop every other month. Meanwhile, his long-suffering wife existed silently in the background.

No wonder she'd gone so dull. It was all her husband's fault!

"I'm sorry, Switz. Ben is stuck in traffic and won't make it—"

The sound of her voice made him jump to his feet. He needed to get out of here.

However, Rio stood in the doorway, blocking his path.

Unless he brushed against her as he made his way past.

Not something he wanted to contemplate. Not now. Not knowing what he knew, with his heart breaking all over again.

He stopped just before the threshold, and she stood there on the other side, all tiny and delicate and breakable. So utterly breakable. She raised those brown eyes flecked with hazel his way. Even they seemed to have turned into murky darkness, shadowed by pain and hurt, their rims looking hollow and gaunt.

He had to curl his hands into fists to stop himself from reaching out for her, from placing his palms gently on her face to then press a soft kiss on her forehead. He'd be tender at first, so she'd know she was safe with him, would always be, before taking her full, pouty lips and showing her the kind of red-hot passion she evoked in him.

One blink. Two, from Rio. "Switz?"

"If—" He took a deep breath, knowing he was unable to stop himself from saying it. "If you were mine, I would never hurt you."

With those words, he stormed out of Tempo and

into the brittle cold of November that came like a welcome 'wake up!' slap to his face.

***

Eighteen months ago ...

Zediah was taking his time strolling on the east side of St John's Wood that early summer evening. Though it got dastardly cold in winter, he still loved London and would miss it when he left for LA in a week.

Over the past few years, he'd realized he was completely into music, way more than any of the politics back home or even the life of a prince. The offer to partner with a world-renowned DJ launching a record label in Los Angeles had seemed like an answer to all his prayers.

He'd done his mandatory two years of national service, had chosen charity work instead of pursuing a military career. If only his family would let him show them all the good spreading music around the world could bring! Duty first, they'd said. Well, his heart wasn't in it.

Actually, his heart belonged to Rio Mittal, but that was also a non-starter. It appeared she had filed for divorce from Gary Bicknell, especially after the splash his affair with an up-and-coming Caribbean singer had made.

From what he'd gathered, public opinion had sided so much with Rio, the starlet's record label had pushed back the release of her first album indefinitely. Rumours of the Mercato when clubs traded players said Ashton Rovers were looking to offload their scandal-mongering left midfielder.

Rio. Under other circumstances, and if he were not on his way to LA, maybe there could've been something.

He slowed in his stroll when a cab drew up a couple houses farther away, and a woman stepped out. As the vehicle drove off, she looked up, and he found himself flummoxed. Rio. She was there, just in front of him.

She seemed just as stunned as he, and she stood there for a few seconds, looking stricken.

"Switz?"

Again, the sound of his moniker coming from her tongue sent a shiver down his spine. He also didn't pick any despondency this time in the word. Just— pleasurable?—surprise.

He jogged the remaining few steps to reach her and couldn't help but smile as he saw her more clearly now. It may be evening, but twilight was still hours away, so the soft ambient light bathed her beautiful features in a gold wash. She looked healthier today, less fragile, more like the woman who had captured his whole being during that party.

"Fancy seeing you here," he found himself saying. Sometimes, he amazed himself with what came out of his mouth around her.

She gave him a soft, sardonic smile. "I live here."

When she nodded towards the house behind her, he laughed. Good one on him.

"What about you?" she asked.

He shrugged. "Just out for a stroll."

She nodded, already starting towards the main gate to the low-built, lateral detached dwelling. With her hand on the latch, she paused, then turned to him.

"Would you like to come in for a drink?"

Every fibre of his body screamed in the affirmative. Yet, a careful part of his functioning brain knew this as a bad idea.

Rio was single now, and though he wasn't a madman who couldn't control himself, he wouldn't make any effort to if she gave her full-blown consent.

"Sure," he heard himself saying. Guess the brain had been overruled.

He followed her down the wide carriage driveway,

the gravel crunching under their feet. She paused to open the front door, then stopped on the threshold just as he was about to enter.

Rio lifted her face to his, and he took in the pretty features that looked a little pinched tonight. Must be due to the swept-back hair she'd pulled tightly away from her face.

The look sure didn't suit her. It was the softness that lit her up, gave her such an aura of delicateness belying her laughing nature and cheerful disposition. He knew in his heart the real her was the woman he had met at the party, not the one at Tempo.

Her lips parted, and his gaze was drawn to the light hint of moisture lingering on them as if she'd just wet them with her tongue. Just imagining it made him grow hard. *Down, boy.*

She kept on staring at him like that for what seemed like ages but must just have been seconds, then she took in a deep breath and stepped inside the house. He followed on her heels, and she didn't break eye contact once.

"Switz," she whispered. "What ... what you said to me back then. You meant it?"

If you were mine, I would never hurt you.

He remembered, all right. "Every word."

The door closed with a push of her hand, and then she was in his arms. She was kissing him, and he was kissing her back, savouring the plush feel of those luscious lips against his, finally. The lean and wiry, yet muscled and strong frame she could move so beautifully pressing against him.

He knew where this was going, and so did she. But he had to be sure.

Forcing himself to break free from her kiss, he stared into her eyes. "Tell me to stay ..."

She huffed, her chest rising and falling with her

heavy breathing.

Then she said it. "Stay."

They kissed again, and somehow, he was being tugged up a sprawling staircase to a level upstairs. Right ahead lay a closed door, and when she pulled him into the adjoining room through the opened doorway, he wasted no time protesting, for he could see a bed in there.

On it, they fell, clothes flying all over the space, lips and hands searching and seeking, exploring, touching, tasting.

Zediah found enough functioning brain cells to reach for his discarded trousers and get a condom before letting lust drive him to finally sink into her.

They soared together, and their climax was so strong, he collapsed on the bed and rolled over onto his side so he wouldn't crush her. After, he had no idea when an exhausted sleep claimed him.

When he woke up, night had clearly fallen, a hint of moonlight bathing the room through the curtains that had not been closed. The bed was empty, though. With a frown, he got up and pulled on his boxers, then padded his way across the carpeted landing to the stairs, taking them to reach the ground level. Something told him it was where she'd be.

Once in the lobby, he glanced around. A drawing room to the left, from where he could see outside, and it was empty. He tried his luck to the right, across the formal dining room, then into an adjoining living room that opened on the back garden. He glimpsed marble counters in the room at the far end, though. Must be the kitchen. Indeed, it was, and he found her there, standing at a French window in a champagne-coloured silk robe and a glass of white wine in her hand.

"Rio," he said softly, not wanting to startle her.

She turned her head swiftly his way, blinked a few

times. Then she shrugged.

"Figured I'd give you a clear coast for when you wanted to leave."

He frowned upon hearing this, but the watery smile accompanying the words told him she was putting on false bravado. He should reassure her, make her feel okay and safe and secure and cherished once again.

"You asked me in for a drink," he said. "Still parched, woman."

She laughed. Well, more like sputtered a little wine, but at least the glow had returned to her face and eyes.

She nodded towards the island. "Help yourself."

He went to the bottle and poured himself some of the Sauvignon Blanc. After taking a sip and finding it too sharp for his taste, he put the glass down and went to her, where she stood in front of the French window. Cool moonlight bathed the garden outside, a silvery sheen on everything it touched, even on the woman before him. Gold suited her much better, though.

The hint of flowery candy-sweet scent tickled his nostrils again this close to her, and he inhaled it in deep, taking his fill. Still, as he stood there taking her in, he reckoned he'd had his drink, even if it had been just a sip. His excuse to remain here had run out.

Taking a deep breath to fortify his resolve, he plunged in. "Do you want me to leave now?"

His heart hammered in his chest as he waited for her answer. She slowly turned towards him, the stemless glass in her hand twirling the wine absently in its depths. Then a soft smile graced her lips.

"No. Stay with me."

His breath came out in a rush—he hadn't realized he had been holding it in. Gently, he drew closer to her and swept her hair to the side to drop a soft kiss on the bared collarbone that seemed to stand out a bit more prominently than before.

Thinking about the hell she'd been through made a pang hit his heart. Her husband's many infidelities must've wreaked havoc on her.

He should've asked her to run away with him that very night. It would've saved her from all this undue hurt.

"Stay with me," she muttered again, right before he claimed her lips and kissed her with all the passion she stirred in him.

When he pulled away, everything inside him was still swirling around. He pressed his forehead to hers, clasped her jaw in his palms. What would it hurt now to tell her how he felt? Nothing. He should do it.

"I've wanted to stay with you ever since the very first evening, Rio. You captured my heart, and I fell in love with you right then in that room."

"Switz ..."

He was about to open his mouth to tell her his real name when he saw the tears coursing down her cheeks.

"Hey," he soothed. "What's wrong?"

Her lower lip trembled when she looked up at him with watery eyes.

"I wish—" she started,

"What?" he asked softly, wiping her tears away with the pads of his thumbs.

"I wish ... you'd taken me away then." Then she looked down and started sobbing so hard, her whole body shook.

"Rio," he murmured, cradling her in his arms.

A quick glance around the room showed him a three-seater sofa in the far corner. Gently, he ambled her there and tried to make her sit. But she was crying so hard, all he could do was pull her to him and settle her in his lap as he sat down.

She cried in silence for a long time, then the words started to flow. He thought he imagined a nightmare at first, but as his horror deepened with everything she said, his own tears unleashed.

Gary calling her Millie had been a twist on the Indian word *imli*, which meant tamarind. He would tease her thus for her dark skin. And while this might be construed as harmless ribbing, the infidelities had been just the half of it. The visible half. Because, when he was alone with her, Gary Bicknell loved nothing more than to use his filthy mouth to demean her more, and then this had escalated to him using his dick—

Zediah couldn't even go there. Rio ... what that man had done to her ... The bastard had thought her consent was a given since she was his wife. Bullshit!

And then something happened amid all this darkness. Rio, pressing her soft lips to the dip of his throat from where she lay in his arms. Her kisses then trailed down to his nipples, his abs. At the sudden stop when she reached the junction of his thighs, he knew what it meant. Her husband had so vilely taken this privilege from her. Zediah would never ask her to do it. Not until she wanted it.

"Babe," he coaxed as he pulled her up gently and brushed the hair from her face. "No. Not like this."

A pleading expression hung in her tearful eyes and in her parted lips. "Don't deny me. Don't deny me yourself."

"Never," he said before claiming her mouth. "But let's do this right."

She nodded softly and let him divest her of the robe, his hands reverently skimming all over her silky-smooth skin.

Zediah kissed her once more. She should be made to feel whole, worthy, like the beautiful goddess she was indeed. With his hands on her waist, he urged her to her knees, making her straddle him. When she broke free and stared into his eyes, he bit his lower lip. She would be the death of him.

"Take me," he said. "All of me."

She did, sinking onto him, guiding him inside her warm femininity, wrecking him in pieces with the soulful manner she took her pleasure from him in the act.

A moan tore from her mouth when she climaxed, and he cradled her to him as she fell, spent, against him, not bothering with his own fulfilment when it came.

Something told him she wouldn't be able to move from here, so he made her wrap her legs around his waist and her arms around his neck, and he carried them back to bed.

Watching her sleeping so peacefully against the cream-coloured sheets, he knew what he had to do. She had his heart; she was his future. He would ask her to come to LA with him, and if she said no, then he'd stay here with her. Damned, be his royal family if they couldn't accept that.

He should leave for Bagumi. The sooner, the better, then he'd just as quickly be able to come back to her.

Just as well, she didn't know he was a prince. He had a feeling he would be coming back to London a mere common man ... and it was perfectly okay by him.

As long as he had her.

***

Present Day

"But why did you tell Dad you were leaving for LA?" Isha asked on the other end of the line.

He didn't know why. He'd asked himself the same question so many times in the past year and a half. Would everything have been different? Would his father not have suffered from a heart attack after Zediah dropped the bombshell that he was leaving Bagumi? If he'd told them he was doing it for love, there might have been a chance.

Then with everything else, the guilt he'd faced. The

recrimination from the rest of the family who saw him as the cause of the king's life-threatening episode had shaken the crown and still bore repercussions today. He'd thought it best to forget about Rio, and she also forget about him.

It had never crossed his mind their second time had been unprotected and could have resulted in a pregnancy. They'd lost so much time, and he might never have known he had a son.

He sighed. "You see, it's all my fault. Don't blame her."

"For sure, I won't. You behaved like such an arse, Zed. Not to mention barging in there asking for your rights!"

He huffed. Just a few moments ago, she had been all gung-ho about *his* rights in the deal. Yet, he knew he should take responsibility for this mess he had created.

"You're gonna have to say sorry, brother. Biiiig time!"

This, he knew. Maybe she could tell him how, though? She was a woman, and she'd know how Rio must've felt when he'd all but bumbled his way through, thinking he was so high and mighty in her office today.

"A little help here?" he asked.

She huffed. "Okay, so here's what you're going to do first …"

CHAPTER FIVE

TUESDAY TURNED out to be one of those days. By noon, Rio was pinching the bridge of her nose and praying for when she'd next be able to down another two tablets of paracetamol. She rarely had such headaches, probably kept at bay thanks to her morning meditation routine.

But peace and mindfulness had flown out the window since Switz's reappearance. So, she'd had to fall on the pills. She still had another three hours to wait, blast it, as she'd taken a dose just an hour ago. It felt like an eternity away!

And where the hell was her assistant? Martha seemed to have melted into the woodwork lately. Rio was hardly able to get the woman in her sights to request a coffee or anything else. What was the matter? Martha had always been able to read her mind before, it seemed. Of course, in her hour of need, everyone would desert her!

Just stop.

Turning into a Bollywood or Zee TV soap opera drama queen would help no one. Tempted as she might be to lie back on the whole 'woe is me' bed, it *was* a bed she had made for herself, after all. No one to blame but her.

A knock came at the door of her office, and she

called for whoever it was to enter.

"I come bearing treats."

A brown paper bag dangled in the air before the person holding it made himself visible. She smiled in reply to Humphrey's wide grin, then breathed in deep when he reached her side and dropped a light kiss on her cheek. It appeared he didn't want to rush things between them—maybe it was how they did it in his world, which, surprisingly, wouldn't be much different from her own traditional one. If Indian mothers had their way, the first kiss between a couple would happen on their wedding night.

Thinking such thoughts caused a shiver to wrack through her. She hadn't been with a man ever since the night Nour was conceived. Not only hadn't she wanted to, what with being pregnant and then having a baby to look after, but no one had stirred her heart, much less her hormones, in all this time.

Still the case. Switz didn't count! She bit her lip. Was she doing Humphrey wrong, going into a relationship with him when she had, at best, tepid feelings for him?

But he didn't seem to mind, did he? He, too, wanted a marriage of convenience that would flow like a tranquil river for the rest of their lives.

Rio was done with trouble, with upheavals, with roller-coasters. Was it too much to ask to be granted some peace?

"Earth to Rio."

She blinked out of her spell to look up into his face. With a soft shake of her head, she smiled. "Sorry. Got lots on my mind."

"These can help."

He shook the paper bag in front of her, and she caught whiffs of sugar and a hint of vanilla. Her suspicions were confirmed when he opened it, and her stomach chose right then to give a loud growl. The two of them looked at each other and burst out laughing. Guess it would be a good thing to eat something. The pain meds she was taking would surely give her an ulcer if she kept up with her unintentional fast.

Propping herself on the edge of her desk, she reached for the paper bag and delved a hand in to retrieve a thin ring of piped dough smothered in powdered sugar. Baked, not fried—the only kind of doughnuts she could eat ever since getting pregnant.

And Humphrey knew it. He'd been there for much of the past year, a friend to her. A rock, despite waiting quietly in the shadows and not pushing her for more—for anything—at any point.

How had she lucked out in finding such a man, much less nabbing him as her own?

She could not let him down ... and she wouldn't.

So she reached up with her left hand and softly clasped his cheek. She should have kissed him, but something inside her knew he was the kind of man who didn't need things to be rushed, who valued consideration more than effusive displays. "Thank you."

He smiled back, his kind smile again, and something in her heart constricted. He was a good man.

"Eat up," he said. "I bet you didn't have any breakfast."

She frowned a little at this but threw his comment off with a laugh. "Why would you say that?"

He raised his eyebrows. "Getting close to Christmas, Rio? Remember last year?"

She groaned and rolled her eyes. He knew her too well. She did, indeed, seem to get caught up in a spiral as the holiday fervour gripped everyone around and even turned the kids into hyperactive bouncy balls of energy and passion. She quickly forgot to eat something substantial when things got busy—a morning smoothie didn't count.

So she forced herself to slow down and savour every bite of those little cakes. There would be some sugar high later and the subsequent crash, but she'd deal with it in due time. Right now, the carbs were a godsend.

Humphrey settled into the visitor's chair, content to let her eat. One more thing she liked about him—he didn't feel the need to fill every silence with empty words. Not like Gary, who had needed to hear himself talk all the time.

As the thought crossed her mind, she stifled the frown trying to seize her features. Why was she thinking of the arsehole now? Gary Bicknell had been good riddance from her life, never more so after Switz Bagumi had so mindfully brought her back to life when he had made love to her. When he had given her reins in their lovemaking—

And she couldn't be thinking of *that*! Not now. Not when she was almost engaged to another man. When Switz himself—Zediah—had stepped back into her world to upturn the fragile semblance of peace, she had managed to weave for herself.

Humphrey got to his feet and placed a hand on her shoulder, which made her jerk softly as her gaze focused on his face.

"You okay?" he asked, concern heavy in his tone. His eyebrows almost met over the bridge of his nose.

Switz—Zediah—might be back, but this should have no bearing on her world. True, he was Nour's father, and that wouldn't change, nor would she try to shift this reality, as unpleasant as it now felt to her. But her future was with Humphrey. Some things were better left unsaid.

She shook her head and gave him a wan smile. "Terrible headache this morning."

"Paracetamol?"

"Just took a thousand milligrams an hour ago. Doesn't seem to be doing its job."

He stayed silent for a few seconds. "Maybe coffee would help?"

She nodded. "If I could find Martha. She seems to have disappeared today."

"Let me go get you some."

She gave him a grateful smile, and her hands flew to her temples once he was out of the room. This headache would be the death of her.

The landline rang, and she reached for it with another scowl. Why hadn't Martha fielded this call? This sure hadn't been patched through.

Still, she answered, and a huge sigh escaped her as soon as she heard the dejected greeting from Mila, one of the teachers.

"Huge pileup near Chalk Farm, Rio. I'm stuck, and there's no parking space where I can leave the car and hop it on foot to you."

She groaned upon hearing this. "Your class starts in ten minutes."

"I know! And I'll get there ASAP, but could you please step in until I get there? Might take me about an hour, hopefully, less."

"Fine," she sighed. A glance at the day's schedule made her stomach bottom out. Mila was scheduled to teach the kids nuevo tango today.

"Cheers. I owe you one."

And she wouldn't let the woman forget! Cutting the call, she heaved another sigh and trudged around the desk to open the bottom drawer.

"Here," Humphrey said as he entered the office. "Coffee."

"Bless you," she muttered, battling with a recalcitrant buckle.

"What are you doing?"

"Changing shoes. Mila is caught in traffic, and I have to step in for her class which starts shortly."

Thank goodness she kept a pair of dance shoes in the office. A relic of her teaching days, but it would still do. As long as the heel didn't break down on her during a routine. But she'd bought a pair which had cost a fortune at the time; it should last a while still.

Next, she reached for the travel cup. She downed a long swig of coffee, welcoming the caffeine that gave her a boost and seemed to sharpen her focus while easing some of the vice holding her forehead captive in its grip.

Getting up and letting herself find a steady stand on the three-inch heels, allowing her weight to spread evenly across her footing, she inhaled deeply. She called forth the teacher who had once lived inside her. It felt like ages ago since she'd last summoned this persona which embodied loose limbs, nimble muscles, and a hefty dose of resilience and patience. Dealing with raucous teenagers and young adults would take their toll on a saint even.

Stopping by Humphrey, she clasped his hand in hers. "Come on. Let's tango."

He laughed. "I doubt it."

They made it to the floor in the adjoining part of the level, and the hoots and hollers started in earnest.

"Miss Rio on da floor!" one of the youths cheered on.

"Can it, Travis," she replied good-naturedly.

It wouldn't do to give this veritable clown an avenue to take the mickey. As one of the longest-standing students in Tempo, he knew her from the first days at the NGO when she'd striven to teach them yoga to open their joints and loosen and strengthen their muscles. She'd then risen through the ranks to become their chief choreographer who had ended up putting together their performance for the foundation's gala three years earlier.

She'd done it to music produced by Switz Bagumi. Yes, with Dilmas, but the original score had been all him, a mix of rhythmic beats that had taken them through Africa and Brazil via Argentina. Her choreography had merged elements of tribal dances with capoeira moves and a sensual tango *canyengue*.

Thrown off-kilter as the thought of Switz assailed her again, she, however, shook herself and urged the students, about a dozen today, to sit on the polished wood of the floor in a semi-circle. At the same time, she explained the fundamentals of tango before segueing into what they were supposed to cover in the lesson.

"So you're saying any music with a good beat can be tango-ed on?" a girl named Clara asked.

"Nuevo tango, yes. You can impress the moves and the complicity on any track. Some might fit better than others, but it is doable," she concurred.

Movement at the back of the room caught in the periphery of her eye, and absently, she raised her gaze. Hopefully, it would be Mila making it in.

Breath got knocked out of her when she saw who now stood in the studio, the front door closing soundlessly behind him.

Switz Bagumi, dressed once again in a tailored suit, the gunmetal grey of the delicate fabric bringing out the quicksilver gleam in his dark eyes even more and making his dark skin gleam softly like the hard outer chocolate on a Mars bar. Another treat she'd had to discard because of how it made her think of this man.

Switz. So gorgeous. And so deceptive ... He brought nothing but disaster.

Yet, she couldn't tear her gaze off him, still finding it hard to reconcile his face with the features that looked so much sharper and even ruthless. He no longer sported the long twisted locs to soften his countenance and bring a playful element to the confidence he still carried like a weapon.

What had happened to make him cut his beautiful hair and turn him into this sharp-tacked character?

Around her, a hush had descended on the group, everyone now looking towards the door. Until Travis jumped up and rushed to hug Switz.

Zediah, she reminded herself. *His real name is Zediah.*

"Switz, my man!" Travis released him to then bump fists.

It looked entirely incongruous to see the suit-clad man who seemed so serious and important, humouring a downtrodden teen from one of the worst council estates in North London. Yet, it also seemed perfectly natural, as though Zediah belonged in this world, maybe even more so than the—corporate? Business? Banking?—universe his clothes lent credence to.

He was a music producer. Maybe he'd risen up the ranks to become a music mogul these days.

Was it the reason he was back now? There had always seemed to be something eating at Switz Bagumi in the past, like a point he needed to prove, to have the world validate. Strangely, this appeared to be gone now.

Would his next step be to take her son away from her because he could? Those clothes screamed money. He must be a man with capable means.

Thoughts of Nour flared a red-hot light in her chest. He'd get to *her* son over her dead body if he ever tried to twist her hand.

"Really?" Clara was exclaiming. "Rio, he's the one who made the epic track for the gala way back?"

Hearing those last words pinched her heart as it really did seem so far away in the past. A lifetime ago, even.

But dozen-plus pairs of eyes were looking at her,

and she better get a grip on herself. "It's true."

And those dark eyes were among the lot, yet she felt them, unlike all the others, boring into her, stripping her bare of her armour, peering straight into her soul. Blinking, she looked away. She didn't need to hold his gaze on top of everything. Not after the way her stomach had spewed out a veritable kaleidoscope of butterflies that had rushed forth to flutter tingles in all parts of her body.

"I'm sorry for disturbing you," Zediah said in a low, almost silky voice.

Could butterflies grow electric, like eels? She would swear volts upon volts of current discharged throughout her system upon hearing his tone. The very same man, who had made her laugh and then soothed her worst nightmare when he had cared for her so sweetly on that night ...

She gulped hard. "It's okay. Just a lesson going on."

The sooner she returned to some semblance of being in control, the better it would be for all of them.

"Yeah," Travis piped up. "Rio's about to teach us how to tango. I still remember the moves from Switz's track, Miss."

Bushy eyebrows rose and fell repeatedly.

Rio could almost see the youth salivating to be allowed into such a tight embrace requiring extreme closeness and sensuality throughout.

"Nice try, Travis. You're not getting your grubby paws on me," she quipped.

Collective laughter shook the room, the lad taking it in stride. His original crush on her way back then had become the stuff of gentle ribbing nowadays.

"Bet Switz still remembers the steps," Travis continued.

Rio pinched her lips hard to stop herself from

swearing. "He just made the music. He wasn't there for the dance."

"But I bet he knows how to tango. Do you, mate?"

The little shit would just not let up, would he?

"I do," Zediah replied ever so softly.

Another gulp to force herself to retain her composure. She did not like where this was going.

"So you two could show us how it's done. You were just telling us any track can be good for a tango, Miss."

Would all her words and action return to bite her in the arse right then?

"I already have a partner," she said and looked to Humphrey.

He, however, raised his hands up as if in surrender. "Two left feet, Rio. You don't want to try your luck."

Yep, just her luck, indeed. She should regain the upper hand. Trying to escape would not help her achieve that. So she stood straighter and cocked her head to the side, her gaze travelling over Zediah's suit-clad form to notice the soft leather brogues on his feet. Blast it—he'd even worn shoes he could dance in.

Fine. She'd so do this. "Switz?"

An eyebrow raised on his picture-perfect face. "A tango?"

"Nuevo Tango," she confirmed with a nod.

"Okay."

As if in slow motion, he reached for the button on his suit jacket and undid it to then shake the garment off his body. Next, he removed the cufflinks at his wrists and rolled up the sleeves of his crisp white shirt to his elbows.

Rio's mouth went utterly dry as she watched him, careful not to let any emotion filter through her non-verbal language. It still looked like he had a fine body underneath the clothes. One she could remember oh-so-clearly if she closed her eyes …

He started in her direction, with a smooth gait and long strides eating the space between them. Finally, he stood before her, and in the heels, she only had to tilt her neck just this slightly to be able to look into his face. With him so up close and a spotlight shining just behind his head, shadows danced on his features.

A lick of apprehension flickered along her lower back. Frankly, she knew nothing about this man. She hadn't even known his real name twenty-four hours earlier. Who knew what he was capable of? While she could say for certain he wasn't a monster like Gary had been, there still existed so many depths about him she hadn't probed or even fathomed.

A gasp hitched in from her parted lips, and his eyes narrowed.

"I would never hurt you."

She blinked. Had he said that? Or was she imagining the words he had spoken to her in these very premises all those years ago? Then, he'd made her imagine, for just a second too long, what it would really be like if she were *his*.

All around them, music started thrumming. A mirthless snort erupted from her when she recognized the track, and across from her, Zediah smiled. An electro-pop hit from Dua Lipa. Seriously? Guess they really would challenge her claim that any music could be used for tango.

As the song finally picked up after its synth bassline opening, they started circling each other, gazes locked, their steps tentative but never hesitant. They gauged each other and read their bodies' energies and vibes along with the feel of the music.

Then the lyrics started, some part of them registering in the back of her head as the rhythm fused with her blood and aligned itself on the tempo her partner set.

Backwards and forward, close and far, shoulders to chest to hips barely touching before moving away, their *abrazo*—the embrace—tight then in a loose V, fluid, natural, an equalitarian exchange where she could choose to follow rather than have his drive imposed on her.

Her hand in his firm grasp, her other palm solidly holding on to his firm, solid shoulder, the heat of skin and blood wrapping them in a cloud of perception where only they existed. Just like that night, on her sofa, when he had allowed her to take her pleasure from him ...

As the singer's voice reached a higher note in the middle eight, building to a crescendo, time seemed to stop. Their bodies touched, her shoulder to his chest as he leaned and tilted to her right, carrying her with him.

Her left foot dragged softly as he pulled her along, and the energy in her left leg urged her to surrender, to stake her claim on him, to let it rise and wrap around his thigh in a natural *gancho*, pulling his pelvis against her softer belly—

A flare of cold realism burst at the very last second. Rio let her leg keep on dragging before she triggered her footwork, allowing her to skilfully pivot and angle her upper body away, all while he still held her hand in his.

What had she been about to do? If she'd gone along with her base instinct, they would have looked like a couple on the verge of sexual intercourse. This could not happen; there was no future for her and Switz. Zediah.

The music still blaring, she steeled herself and let her body flow into the moves they'd already performed at the repeating chorus. All the while, she kept a close eye on his feet. Anticipating a *sacada* whereby he would displace her legs by stepping into her space and thus claim the upper hand, take back control.

But this never happened, and as the song ended and an anti-climactic silence resonated in the hushed studio, Rio tore her gaze from Zediah's and stepped away from him. As whoops and hollers started, she caught sight of Mila stepping into the room in a frenzied rush.

Great. She'd done her part—now she could run away to her office as the teacher picked things up here.

She didn't bother with the joyous exclamations, didn't even stop when she heard someone saying they'd caught the dance on video. What had she done? And in front of Humphrey, no less.

Horror filled her. She reached out and quickly grabbed his hand as she went past him, tugging him with her to her office. She slammed the door shut behind her and stood there facing him with her heart running a mile a minute and tears clouding her eyes. She'd already fucked up her life twice—she couldn't let this happen again. But she would respect his decision, whatever it turned out to be.

"I—" She swallowed the lump in her throat and blinked hard. "I will understand if you decide to not go to the gala with me now."

From the get-go, it had been code between them for the relationship they'd build from that point forward.

Humphrey frowned. "Why would I do that?"

So she'd need to spell it out for him. Guess it never would be easy for her. Well, so be it.

She waved towards the studio floor. "The dance … That man …"

Try as she wanted, she couldn't bring herself to say more.

"He's Nour's father, isn't he?"

No point playing coy and asking how he knew. "Yes."

"Do you want him back into your life?"
"No."

Not when she had already committed herself to

another man. She wasn't a kind of flighty butterfly who would enjoy nothing more than to flit about in a dangerous love triangle. It exhausted her just to read about such tropes, especially in those YA books.

"Then it's settled."

She peered up and glanced into his face, which didn't look any more worked up than usual. "So you'll just take me at my word?"

"Isn't your word good enough?" he asked with a smile, which let her know he was teasing.

"It is! But I don't want you to think—"

"That you might be unfaithful?"

"I'll never do that to you," she muttered, voice thick with unshed tears.

"I know. I saw it."

She blinked. "What?"

Humphrey chuckled. "I might have two left feet, but it doesn't mean I didn't learn how to dance, and ballroom, too. That moment right there, when the music reached a crescendo, everything seemed to indicate when he was dragging you along that your next move would be a *gancho*. Yet, you didn't do it because you know what it means."

A part of her had done so for pure self-preservation, but she'd also recalled she wasn't a free woman who could just give in to her urges. Humphrey had read it all in her moves.

What about Zediah? Had he picked the same message up?

And speak of the devil—a knock came at her door, his low voice calling out her name just after.

"You should speak to him," Humphrey told her softly.

"Don't want to," she mumbled, petulant.

He laughed as he drew closer and placed his warm palms on her shoulders. "He's still Nour's father. Unless he's a monster, your son should get to know him."

She could do nothing else but nod at his words.

"Good," he said. Then, with a soft kiss on her forehead, he let her go and exited the office, leaving the door ajar behind him.

It would be up to her to take the next step now. So, fortifying herself with a deep breath, Rio stepped towards the doorway and pulled the panel wide open.

"Zediah," she clipped out. "Come on in."

When he got in, and she closed the door behind her, she didn't bother to look up before firing her first question.

"What are you doing here?"

She'd been dreading this, she now reckoned, ever since he'd left this same space the previous day. Hence the headaches and the need for so much paracetamol, not to mention the sleepless night she'd tried to sweep away under layers of concealer. He knew how to reach her, whereas she had no clue. Once again. Would it be the tone of their relationship every time?

"Rio, I ... I came to say I'm sorry."

That was rich.

"And these words change what, exactly?" The tart retort had flown out of her lips before she'd even thought it through.

He remained silent for long seconds, then those strong, solid shoulders encased once again in shirt and suit jacket rose and fell in a shrug.

"Nothing, I know," he murmured.

It suddenly dawned on her that if they were to keep up with this blame game—well, if *she* were—they'd be at it for hours. Time she didn't have to lose, and especially not to invest in a battle which would do nothing but bring her down and cast her heart in pain and her soul in darkness. Were it just her? It would've posed no problem to go down this route. Nothing a few pints of Häagen-

Dazs couldn't cure. But she was a mother, with a son to think about, to prioritize.

"Zediah," she started.

"I really am sorry, Rio. For the way I acted yesterday. And also for ... for leaving like I did."

She didn't say a word in reply. Too busy trying to stave off the hurt, every time she allowed herself to recall how he had let her down after showing her the world could be a safe, beautiful place again.

"I was going to come back, you know. That's why I didn't leave a note." He sighed. "I was going back home to Bagumi to speak to my parents about us."

A little throb started in her heart, gaining momentum with every millisecond passing. "Us?"

He nodded. "Yes. I was supposed to leave for LA a week later anyway. I was going to ask you to come with me. If you'd said no, I would've stayed in London. As long as I had you."

She bit her lip hard as the swell of tears grew in her throat. *You had me, Switz. All of me.*

But not anymore. She shouldn't ever forget it.

"So that's where you've been all this time. In LA."

"Bagumi," he corrected. "My father had a heart attack when I ... told him I wouldn't be moving back home."

"When you told him about me, you mean." She wasn't African, Black, or of the same religion as he— interracial couples almost never got a happy ending in Bollywood or real life.

"I didn't tell them about you. I didn't get a chance to. Trust me, Rio, I wanted to come back to you. I wanted to let you know what had happened."

"And they don't have international phone lines in Bagumi?"

He could've called—he'd always known how and where to find her. Instead, he had just slunk away in the night.

"I'm sorry," he said. "I know I don't deserve it, but I'm here asking for a second chance."

She frowned. "At what?"

"Everything," he added so softly, she again felt she'd imagined the word.

He couldn't be serious. Eighteen months too late, offering too little now. She was turning her life around for good this time.

Their time had come and gone. Yet, it had also left an indelible trace, something phenomenal they'd created together.

Taking a deep breath even as her heart sawed itself in two. Everything inside her remembered loving this man only to have it all burn to cinders. She drew strength from the fact that Humphrey waited for her somewhere in the building. And he trusted her without fail. She should—and would—be building on this kind of feeling instead of fleeting love, which came with a lot of sorry.

"I can't, Switz."

His nostrils flared as he took in her response. His jaw worked as if words wanted to come out but couldn't, then he looked up and caught her eyes with his.

"Can I at least get to know our son?"

"I'll never deny you that." She gulped down hard. "But you're never, ever taking him from me."

"I wouldn't even dream of it. He's yours first, Rio."

At this, she nodded, glad they'd made it clear. His tone had rung with certainty, and her gut, which she'd started to trust on a more visceral level ever since she'd become a mother, told her he wasn't lying.

Good. She'd introduce him to Nour. No time like the present, right?

"Got anywhere you need to be?" she asked.

"No. Why?"

"Then come with me."

CHAPTER SIX

ZEDIAH COULDN'T quite believe it as he watched the scenery change at a plodding, traffic-laden pace when they left Camden to draw closer to the heart of London. Rio was taking him to see his son!

He'd been stunned speechless when she'd replied, "To see Nour," after he'd questioned her request to come along with her. Stupefaction had made him numb at the same time a flurry of explosive fireworks had started all through his gut to spark relentlessly around his heart at the prospect.

He had indeed followed behind her, dogging her steps as she went to grab her coat and then on a search for her PA, Martha. They found her at a table in the Mess room having a cup of tea with the pasty-faced bloke who had been hovering over Rio all along.

Something had been happening there, especially how the blond woman's laughter had died, and her face had scrunched up upon seeing her boss. A woman plus a man alone in a room—it had looked dodgy.

A pointed glance at the man had, however, alleviated any desire to slam his fist in the guy's face if he were doing wrong by Rio. He'd been courteous and considerate with her, nothing in his behaviour appearing shady.

Zediah's frown had morphed into something a tad

more like preoccupation. He'd witnessed Rio exchange a few words with the man, then gently pat his shoulder before leaving the room without a backward glance.

What was going on between them? Surely, if they'd been involved, she would've kissed him, or at least done more than just a fleeting, almost impersonal touch before she left.

He should cool his heels. Rio might not even want to think of a second chance with him, but Zediah could be very patient when the need arose. And if he had to win her from another man—as he should have the first time—he would do it.

He dismissed the thought as he breathed in the heated air inside the Range Rover Evoque. The scenery puzzled him. That was Hyde Park, wasn't it? And here were the crisp white, terraced stucco townhouses of Belgravia. And there was Cadogan Square, if he wasn't mistaken.

Why were they here? Taking a detour towards Southall? But it would've been easier to take the streets outside of central London rather than cut through these affluent neighbourhoods.

A sense of unease gripped him and soured his stomach. He'd been ignoring it ever since he had come out of the building where Tempo was housed and had found Rio striding towards the side garage. More perplexingly, the luxury SUV parked there.

He'd dismissed it as maybe a perk of the job. But Rio worked for an NGO.

This kind of money would've been put to better use for running the place, not to give the Executive Director this type of wheels.

Then they turned into a narrow street. The terraced houses' fronts a mix of white-washed walls, luxury dark grey trimmings, and sand-coloured brick façades, a few potted plants in front of the doors, window baskets of colourful flowers just barely hanging on still in the winter.

When the car stopped in front of one dwelling with a brown brick frontage and black doors, he recognised the place for what it was. Mews. And in Knightsbridge, no less.

It suddenly dawned on Zediah how much of an absolute bloody idiot he had been. Rio drove a Range Rover vehicle, and she'd just brought him to her home. The place where his son lived. One of the classiest neighbourhoods in London, with Buckingham Palace just a stone's throw away and some of the best schools in the land within spitting distance.

Here he'd been thinking he would find her down on her luck, struggling to make ends meet. He would swoop in as the regal saviour to rescue her from this life of drudgery and provide all the best opportunities possible for his child.

How wrong had he been? She'd already been doing a damn fine job of it, it appeared. She hadn't needed him.

She *didn't* need him ...

And this realization hurt. Because he'd always thought of himself as her knight in shining armour. Except, she had never been a damsel in distress. She'd single-handedly worked her way out of the pit without any help, none less from him.

She stopped and opened the car door. Zediah snuck a sideways glance and fell in love with her all over again.

Just like that.

Everything she was, everything she embodied. It tore at his heart, making the place she'd held there from the very first moment grow as if it were a terrestrial fault line that would forever keep on widening.

A knock came at his window, and he shrugged out of his thoughts, opened the door and got out. Rio was looking at him with a weird frown as if she were gauging him up.

"Last chance, Zediah. If you don't want to do this, say so now."

How could she even fathom something like this? It was his son—his flesh and blood—they were talking about here.

"Never," he replied softly. "Let's do this."

"It'd be good if you didn't look so much like a deer caught in headlights. Nour doesn't bite." A chuckle escaped her. "Well, not much."

He blinked. "What?"

She laughed again, then turned towards the black-panelled front door. "Come along."

He followed her in, a wave of soft scent like lavender—mixed with baby powder—wafting up and settling over him like a cloak of peace and serenity. He shouldn't dread this—and he wasn't, as dread wasn't the word he'd use—but everything inside him converged to let him reckon life as he'd known it would never be the same again, not after these next moments.

"Oksana?" Rio called softly.

"We're upstairs," came a shouted reply.

"Great. Means he's awake. Follow me," she said.

She went inside, going to the far right of the open-plan ground floor. He caught glimpses of a fireplace in a massive reception area with a kitchen bordering to the right and a set of staircases beside it.

Not too shabby, and he was putting it mildly. What a fool he'd been! No wonder she'd been ready to chuck him out of her office that first day. He should count himself lucky she was even letting him see their son.

They took the stairs to one level up, where she turned left and undid the child-safety swing door barring the doorway to a big bedroom. He could already see an array of soft colours on the walls and a crib to the side.

He'd told himself he was prepared for this. He would've bet money on it, even. But the first actual sight of his son ... His step faltered, his body froze, and his heart? It swelled and grew and exploded all to build itself back up once more and start the process all over again.

Time stood still for him while he gazed at the grinning baby who lurched onto his stomach, attempting to happily crawl towards his mother.

"Mamamama!"

Rio laughed and crouched to grab him into her arms and place resounding kisses on the chubby cheeks, making the kid squeal happily.

That—it was the sound of joy. Pure. Unadulterated. Just pristine and perfect.

Like this child was.

His child.

"Zediah, this is Oksana, Nour's nanny."

He vaguely recalled seeing a young blonde in the periphery, and after a few hushed words from Rio, the girl left them and went downstairs.

By now, it was just them. Him, Rio, their son.

How it should have been ever since she'd found out she was pregnant.

How it should be from here on.

Nothing else mattered. Not his family, his title, the crown. He'd give it all up in a heartbeat for a chance at a whole life with this baby ... and this baby's mother.

As he gulped back, a lump blocking his throat all of a sudden, his eyes started burning, and he blinked hard, registering too late a tear had fallen down his cheek.

"Come on, don't be shy," Rio was saying.

To him, apparently. He should go in, introduce himself to his lad. Glancing down, he noticed she'd left her shoes outside the room on the landing. He proceeded to divest himself of his brogues and then walked into the nursery.

It felt like he was tiptoeing or even walking with those gigantic, no-gravity leaps the American astronauts had taken on the moon. Little by little, the distance between him and Rio decreased, his vision tunnelling right along until all he could see was this woman and the child she had borne to him.

Nour. As much as his mother was a burst of radiance, the boy was indeed a ray of bright light. He looked adorable, too, though Zediah was undoubtedly biased. But he'd seen his lot of babies. Nour painted a terribly cute picture with his smooth skin, chubby cheeks, bow-shaped mouth, pert nose, big doe eyes, and a thatch of soft curls that made the gentlest of halos around his head.

Zediah was no expert, but he would venture a guess the baby was a bit on the tall side already, what with the limbs that looked more long than fleshy.

He must have stopped and stared for ages, and Rio had let him.

"Do you want to hold him?" she asked, finally breaking the loaded silence between the two adults. The baby squealed and babbled away with his nonsensical chatter.

He blinked, finally focusing on her again. And he could all at once see the resemblance. Nour was indeed his mother's son. Were it not for the slightly darker skin tone and the curls, he seemed to have nothing of his father.

A pang clamoured in his gut as a hand crushed his heart in a vise.

He didn't deserve to be here today, did he? After the way he'd behaved, how he had let them both down ...

The child lurched in his direction, the decision taken out of his hands, forcing him to surface from his doldrums. Every instinct rushed forward to catch the suddenly moving bundle. Nour's face landed softly against his shoulder, and Zediah's arms came up to hold him tightly. His hands landed on Rio's—she still had the child safely, thank goodness.

"Got him?" she asked.

He couldn't help but think she was asking about more than the moment, and he wanted to answer that yes, he did. He got them both forever from here on.

But the only thing to make it through was a nod. She pressed the warm, soft, and squirming mass into his chest, making sure he had one arm under the squishy nappy-covered little butt and the other braced against the boy's upper back.

When she let go, he tightened his hold, afraid he'd let the child fall or slip from his grip, though remaining careful to also not hurt this fragile creature.

"Shouldn't I be holding his neck or something?" he asked.

Rio laughed. "Only when they can't hold their heads upright. We're past that stage now."

They were, and he had missed it all. He imagined the moment Rio would've come up to him and either told him she was pregnant or shown him the pregnancy test strip with its two pink lines like they did in the movies. He could feel the joy that would've burst through his heart, the love that would've engulfed him for this woman. How he would've kissed her and then reverently touched her belly, pressing a kiss near her navel and already speaking to the little bean growing in there.

He would have started to count the days on the calendar for when their baby would be born. He would've looked after her, made sure she ate only organic food and went to all her check-ups and scans. Gotten out at three in the morning to find her whatever craving would've taken hold of her during those nine months.

Alas, they hadn't had that because of him.

If it took his whole life to make up for it, he would willingly give it. No one else deserved it more than these two here.

"You're allowed to talk to him, you know," Rio quipped.

Zediah chuckled.

"Hey," he murmured to the kid.

"Want to tell him who you are?" she prompted.

He blinked, tearing his eyes from his son, who had been staring at him all this time. Probably just seconds that felt like an eternity. Babies just did not have this kind of attention span, did they?

"You sure?" he asked her softly.

She simply nodded. He thought he saw a wash of sorrow flit over her face to darken her features, but it was gone in a flash when she looked back at the baby.

Zediah snuck in a deep inhale and peered into the brown eyes with flecks of hazel blinking up at him as if with avid curiosity and asking, '*Who the heck are you?*'

"Hi, Nour." The kid appeared to perk up upon hearing his name. "I'm ... I'm your dad."

That title. The world hadn't come crashing down. A tsunami hadn't washed away all the coastlines. Every volcano on the planet hadn't erupted.

But in Zediah's mind, it felt as if all of it had indeed happened. The Earth had tilted on its axis when he'd said the word.

Nour stared at him for another second, then the little face scrunched up before it fell smack against his shoulder, the tiny mouth munching on the fabric of his suit jacket. When Zediah looked, he could indeed see a wet stain building there in the material.

Rio laughed next to him. "You've been accepted."

He blinked. "What?"

She tilted her head towards where their son was savagely trying to eat into his suit. "He's just started teething and is very picky with what he chooses to put into his mouth. He just showed you he likes you."

A sigh of relief escaped him, even though he frowned a little at the renewed toothless vigour being unleashed on his jacket. But it was a good start, right, his son liking him? While he ...

The lump returned to his throat again, and he cleared it softly.

"I— I love him," he muttered, then scrutinised her face. "Rio, I love him so much already."

Was she blinking away tears? But she gave him a trembling smile and nodded. "I loved him from the first moment I saw him, too."

"So this is normal?"

"It should be, anyway." Then she shook her head and reached for the baby. "Best we occupy him with an actual teething toy unless you can afford to have that suit ruined."

He was reluctant to give the child back, but he relented and let go once he was sure Rio had him safely in her grip. A wave of cold washed over him—Nour's tiny body had been so warm against his, he felt the temperature change even though the heating was well on in the nursery. And the farther Rio moved away with the child, the more an icy draught settled in her wake.

Yet, she'd only stepped a few feet away to the giant playmat on the floor where she deposited the baby.

Next, she handed him a squeaky giraffe toy which went promptly into the feral mouth. The same mouth looked like butter wouldn't melt but attacked the poor animal's long neck like it wanted to tear the life out of it.

As he stood there and watched, the tunnel vision returned, and this time, it bade nothing good as he could acknowledge the beginning of a panic attack. Just the mere thought of not having Nour in his sights ... He couldn't think this way, though. Nour belonged with his mother, and Zediah would take all the crumbs she'd let him have. It hardly meant she'd ask him to share in their son's life twenty-four-seven right away.

Forcing himself to regulate his breathing, he brought himself back from the brink and reasoned with himself. Nothing else but Nour mattered now. And Rio, too. Whatever he got from them, he would take, and it would be enough. The form this would take, he had no idea, but he would go with the flow.

Rio looked up then, catching his eye.

"So what now?" he made himself ask, bracing for her conditions. He would listen carefully, respect all her wishes, give her the due courtesy and consideration he had so blatantly denied her all this time.

She gave him a soft shrug. "I guess we take every day as it comes?"

Not ideal, but better than what he'd prepared for. "Fine by me."

***

They did just that in the end. Friday came and found him once again at her house. He had come there every morning after breakfast and left before dinner when Rio got home from work. He'd hoped she'd ask him to stay and eat with them, but so far, she hadn't, and he wouldn't press. Time enough for everything else in the future.

Thinking of the future reminded him of Bagumi and his 'duties' awaiting him there, none less the impending arranged marriage to Bilkiss.

Bagumi was one bridge he wouldn't cross until he absolutely had to. His conversations with his mother on the phone had been succinct, with him evading the topic of his return. He just had to mention something about

Nour to the queen, and he was off the hook.

He'd play the card for however long it would work. For the time being, he enjoyed spending time getting to know his son, who had turned out to be a little hellion who reminded him a lot of Zareb. A warm friendship also developed with Oksana, who had been showing him the ropes of how to cope with said little hellion.

He rose when Rio walked into the nursery that afternoon, hours ahead of her usual arrival time.

"I should get going," he said, though everything inside him screamed to be allowed to stay and spend as much time as possible with his son.

"No, Zediah, don't." Rio shook her head with a sigh. "I'm on my way out again. Well, as soon as I get ready. You should stay," she added with a smile.

He acquiesced with a nod. Settling down on the floor, he absently shook a stuffed elephant in his hand to try and distract Nour, who was sitting on his play mat with an array of toys strewn around him. Oksana was preparing the baby's dinner, so the task of distracting the kid had fallen to him.

So Rio was going out later? A sinking feeling like a boulder being dropped into his gut anchored him to the spot as a thought crossed his mind. Was she going out on a date?

A sharp pain to his knee tore him out of his reflections. "Ow!"

He narrowed his eyes on the wooden cube lying in front of him and looked up just in time to see another block flying in his direction. He caught the thing in mid-air, Nour blinking at him and looking puzzled that his projectile hadn't reached its aim.

The full, pouty lower lip started to tremble, and Zediah sighed. Another crying outburst. He should try to stave it off, by any means. In the few days he'd been here, he already knew what would work without fail.

Though Rio and Oksana would both skewer him with disapproving looks full of reproach if he went along with it.

But he'd be damned if he'd sit here being target practice for a baby who had demonstrated superb aim. Despite having just acquired the ability to throw things more than two inches in front of him.

He stood then scooped the baby in his arms and made his way to the adjoining bedroom and the flat-screen TV on the wall. Switching it on all while bouncing the whining kid on his hip, he used the remote to access YouTube. Now to find some content that would take Nour's attention away from trying to punish his dad for having been such an absent jerk in his mother's life.

The first recommendation would work. But there was only so much Peppa Pig a man could take weekly, and one episode viewed was one too many. Quick—had Nour even seen the thumbnail?

Then something caught his eye, making him smile. The perfect thing to distract his son. He would never publicly admit he was also indulging just as much as the kid in this, though. So he started the clip and plopped down on the thick rug in front of the bed with Nour sitting between his stretched-out legs.

As the cartoon character's weird laugh filled the air, Nour went still, then started giggling right along. Perfect—objective achieved, *and* he'd dislodged Peppa Pig from the top spot, too.

"SpongeBob?" Rio asked as she stopped on the threshold. "Seriously?"

Zediah shrugged, more so since the sight of her had snapped all his vocal cords. She'd dressed in an emerald-green swirly cocktail dress that sheathed her lithe body like an expensive glove. Thin diamante straps crisscrossed over her muscled shoulder blades, meeting the fabric of the garment just above the swell of her delectable backside at the small of her back. Four-inch stiletto heels elongated her legs to almost-stratospheric lengths. She'd pulled her thick hair into a complex updo with some loose locks artfully framing her face.

He, however, zoomed in on the thin strand that had broken free to softly curl against the nape of her neck. His fingers itched to wrap the hair around his index while he caressed her silky skin with his knuckles and made her shiver with desire.

Nour gurgled something from below, and Zediah tore his gaze from the magnificence that was Rio to see the baby also seemed to be approving the woman's elegant attire.

"Ooh, fancy," Oksana said as she brushed past into the room. "Did you use the hairspray I gave you?"

"How do you think this whole thing hasn't fallen flat already?" Rio replied.

The nanny picked the baby up and started for the door again. When she drew close, Nour tried to reach for the sparkling chandelier earrings dangling from his mother's ears. Rio easily side-stepped with a laugh and, blocking the jewels with her hands, bent to kiss Nour's cheek. The two women then started towards the stairs, going down to the main level. Zediah got up to follow them.

"Don't wait up," Rio was saying. "I might not get home until the early hours of the morning."

A lance of burning jealousy slashed through his chest. Looking so beautiful, she was obviously going on a date. And the mention of early morning? She would most certainly be spending the night with the man who would be accompanying her.

She had a life. He needed to remind himself. That she'd given him a place in their son's existence didn't mean she had opened the doorway to hers.

Yet, all his life, he had been waiting for someone

like Rio. No other woman had made him feel the way she did. Ever. She filled him with desire, with want, made him crave her so severely. Then still, he'd gone and bungled it all up.

The heat of jealousy intensified, wearing him down.

Padding softly to the front window, he stayed a few paces behind the gauzy voile curtain. He would be undetectable from the road yet still able to see her getting into the waiting car. A Rolls Royce Phantom, no less, and as she exited the house, the passenger door opened and out stepped the same insipid blond from Tempo decked out in a tuxedo, with a cummerbund and all. They were definitely off to a fancy event.

So, this was the kind of life she wanted? He should drop the bombshell that he was a bona fide prince—it would surely go a long way in presenting him in a positive light.

Except, he had never used his royal status for anything. Had even abhorred doing so, too. He wouldn't start now when it would mean winning her attention via a method he despised. She deserved so much more.

With a heavy heart, he watched them get into the vehicle and take off. It was a bit like looking at the princess of a fairy-tale riding away into the sunset in her pumpkin carriage with her prince. Too bad he wasn't the actual royal in the reference.

A heavy sigh tore out of him, and he ran a hand over the tight nape of his neck. He should cut his losses when he still could. Returning upstairs, he got his shoes, and he was grabbing his coat from the pegs in the front hallway when Oksana tore the lined wool from his hand.

"No way. You are not leaving. I've got a full marathon of *The Masked Singer* planned tonight, and you're staying. You analyse the music so well."

A groan escaped him.

"Come on," she pleaded. "I'm making popcorn. And

it's not the crap that comes from a microwave."

Zediah smiled. What did he have waiting for him back in the Park Place house? Probably a marathon of the same show—Oksana had indeed got him hooked during the past week. They could definitely watch it together.

"How can I say no to popcorn?" he said with a nod.

"Exactly. Come on, let's feed Nour, grab some dinner, then the sooner I can give him his bath and get him to bed, the sooner we can get started."

It sounded like a solid plan for the evening, except things didn't turn out that way. An hour into his sleep, Nour woke up with a plaintive wailing that all but ripped Zediah to useless scraps.

"Teething pains," Oksana told him calmly. She wasted no time getting the bottle of baby paracetamol syrup and feeding Nour a dose.

As the medicine slowly started working, the crying lessened, settling into an absolutely desolate whinging often accompanied by hiccupping sobs. Zediah, now just a bundle of shreds barely tacked together, wished he could do something, anything, to help ease the plight of his son.

The child felt a little bit warm to him. "Shouldn't we be going to see a doctor? Like at A&E?"

Oksana rolled her eyes at him. "His temperature is just a little over thirty-seven. It's not even considered fever until it's reached thirty-eight, you know."

Still, the low lament was tearing at every layer of his heart. "What can we do for him?"

"He's had the meds. Now we just have to distract him and soothe him until he falls asleep again."

"Should we call Rio?"

This earned him a glare, and he muttered a soft apology. Oksana was a competent nanny. Rio wouldn't leave their son with her otherwise.

They took turns during the evening cradling the baby and pacing the room while the show's reruns stored on the DVR played ahead on the TV. Nour dozed off from time to time against a shoulder, constantly waking with a jerk when they'd try to put him down in his cot, and the weeping would start anew.

By one in the morning, the two of them were utterly exhausted, with Nour giving no sign he would let up.

"What can we do?" a harried Zediah asked for the hundredth time.

"He wants his mummy," Oksana replied.

"We should call her, tell her to come home."

The nanny remained silent, then nodded. "She should be on her way back. These things never go on for too long usually."

Zediah's nostrils flared as jealousy piqued him again. "Didn't you hear her? She said not to wait up."

Blue eyes full of reproach narrowed on him.

"Rio is a good mother, Zediah. Her son always comes first."

The wind tore out of his sails at her scathing tone. "That's not what I meant."

"Good. Because where were you all this time, huh? She's much too good a person to tell you what hell her life has been like all this time, but I'm telling you. You have absolutely no right to question that woman's love and dedication for *her* child."

Chastised, he stayed mum. Though her words made him curious. "What happened to her?"

Oksana grimaced. "Not my place to tell."

The sound of a car engine starting outside made them both go silent. The front door opened and closed softly, then quick footsteps trudged up the stairs.

Rio rushed to the baby in Oksana's arms and placed a gentle hand against his cheek.

"Poor sweetheart," she mumbled. "Teething pains

again?"

Oksana concurred, bringing her up to speed.

Rio nodded. "Let me go get changed first."

With a quick dash, she left the room and went upstairs to the master suite. Less than two minutes later, she was back, the dress having been discarded for loungewear. She reached for the baby right away, and Nour went willingly into her arms, burrowing his face into her neck. Already, the crying had diminished.

"I've got him," she told the nanny. "Go to bed. You have an early morning coming up."

Oksana nodded and left the room, going downstairs to her studio in the basement. Rio rocked the child softly and went into the nursery. She didn't seem to have noticed he was still there. He should let her know he was leaving, but right now, the priority was soothing their son back to sleep.

When he made it into the adjoining room, he found her lying against the many soft pillows arranged like a Turkish lounge in a corner. Nour lay sprawled over her stomach and chest, a tiny fist clenched around a lock of her hair that had fallen across her shoulder.

The soft jersey jumper she'd worn had slipped down one arm and bared the creamy golden skin of her collarbone. Seemed to him the bones weren't so obvious anymore—pregnancy must have made her put on some weight. It suited her.

She looked up when he came in, though nothing in her demeanour indicated any reaction. He should remember this while he still had the hots for her, she clearly didn't anymore.

When he took a few steps in and reached the lounge area as if an invisible magnet behind her had been pulling him all along, she gave him a soft nod. He took it as an invitation to sit down on the cushions by her side.

Watching her gently running her hand over Nour's

back, it struck him how unruffled she appeared.

"It broke my heart to see him crying like this," he ventured.

She nodded. "You, unfortunately, get used to it. All the same, it still fells you every single time."

"You've dealt with a lot of that before?"

"Not teething, but for the first three months, he would have the most awful colic every evening around six, and the only thing that worked was holding him like this."

So she'd had practice. He hadn't, as he hadn't been here.

Oksana's pointed words also made themselves known, and he squirmed. Now was as good a time as any to have a heart-to-heart talk with Rio. There hadn't been a quiet moment for just the two of them lately.

Zediah took a deep breath. "I'm sorry, Rio."

She simply cocked an eyebrow.

"For everything," he added. When she still didn't answer, he knew he should give more. "I meant what I told you the other day. I was going to come back."

"Then your father had a heart attack."

He gulped. "Yes. Because of me."

"He's better now?"

Her solicitude surprised him. Not because he hadn't expected empathy from her, but she was still thinking about someone else's wellbeing when she had also paid a price here.

"Yes," he bit out.

"Are you an only child?"

"Why would you think so?"

"Well, if he took your news this badly, it must mean he had been worried about losing you."

A mirthless chuckle escaped him. Not even close to the truth.

Rio was watching him with a puzzled look on her

111

face.

He shook his head. "I've got three sisters and three brothers, one of whom is my twin."

"Wow."

"Yeah."

"You're identical?"

At this, he laughed. "Thank goodness, no."

"Why not?"

"Well, let's just say he's had a stick up his arse since we were kids."

She laughed, too. "Your father's the traditional type."

"How'd you know?"

"Because a heart attack is also what would happen to my mother if I told her I was moving to another country." She then stayed silent for long seconds. "They rubbed it in, didn't they? That it was all your fault?"

Zediah's throat seized up. He'd never expected anyone to understand what he had gone through in the past year and a half. Yet here was this gorgeous, amazing, wonderful woman who had figured it out without him needing to say a thing. Wordlessly, he nodded.

Her silence seemed to mean she'd acquiesced. A part of him still roiled and churned with the unfairness of it all, for her.

"I should have come back," he said softly.

A soft snore tore through the air. Their gazes went to the baby, who had finally fallen into a deep sleep.

When Zediah looked back up, the depths of hurt and suffering in Rio's eyes made him want to weep. It was like seeing her beautiful irises as dull and muddied as they'd been when he'd seen her at Tempo again all those years ago. And this time, he was the one who'd put all the pain there ... when he'd promised he would never hurt her.

"What can I do to make it right?" he asked, a hitch in his voice.

She gave him a sad smile. Her silence seemed to say it was a tad too late for that.

"Please," he begged.

She tore her gaze away, and her throat worked as she swallowed hard. When she turned to him again, resignation had tightened her features and made her look older, tired.

"It's not just me, Switz."

The use of his nickname squeezed the vice in his chest.

"I managed to turn my life around. Others weren't so lucky."

He blinked. "What?"

"See? You didn't even realize, did you?" A long sigh poured out of her. "Remember Jalil?"

He did. Now. Bile rose in his throat at the reckoning. "What happened to him?"

She shrugged. "Back on the estate, failed his A-levels. Probably embroiled in some gang or the other there."

Her voice hardened with every word. Each successive one drove a blow deep into his gut as if he were being sucker-punched.

Jalil had been a regular at Tempo back when he had produced the music for the foundation gala. The lad had had talent up to his armpits, and Zediah had known he would be the next big thing in a couple of years.

He'd encouraged the kid to pursue his love of music and DJ-ing. Rio had been the sensible voice in the background, advising Jalil to finish his schooling since he'd had the brains for it and then pursue his heart's desire.

Right before he was to leave for LA, Jalil had become something of an unofficial protégé. He'd even planned to bring the youngster over to California once everything was settled and get him started.

Then things had gone haywire. He'd imagined the voice of reason would've prevailed, and Jalil would've finished school and then probably gone on to university as he was that bright.

"I can right this," he told her softly.

It was his fault, and he owed the kid now.

Just like he owed her and Nour.

"Can you?"

Her softly voiced question drove daggers into his soul when it made him contemplate what he could achieve.

"I'll stay and make it all right this time."

The words had torn out of him without a second thought. That's what he had to do. Let his father disown him. Rio didn't need his money or his status, and what he could offer Jalil was entirely his own, with no ties to the crown of Bagumi. His penance could also be to provide such opportunities to other kids who might need them, too.

Yes, it's what he would do.

"What if your father gets sick again?"

"It won't be my fault."

And he suddenly reckoned it hadn't been his fault the first time, either. Parents weren't supposed to bring children into the world and force them to their own ideals of life and expectations.

Looking at Nour, he knew that wasn't how it worked. While it would hurt his ego if his son turned his back on music or anything artistic when he grew up, he would give Nour the freedom to be his own person. Whether he was straight, gay, non-binary, or horror of all horrors, gifted for military strategy, he would respect it.

"It *wasn't* your fault," she concurred in a soft tone.

She understood. Riona 'Rio' Mittal was the only person in the world who 'got' him.

How had he let her go?

Better yet, how should he beg and grovel for a place in her life again, in her heart?

Did he even have a chance? The memory of her slipping into the car earlier blazed inside his head. The bloke's hand on the small of her back, even if it had been over her plush coat. The bright smiles on their faces as they'd greeted each other.

To imagine the other guy touching her, holding her, feeling her warm and supple body in his arms and against him like in the tango they had shared the other day. He didn't even allow the thought into his mind as it would burn him to ashes.

Zediah took the hardest gulp of his life before asking the question plaguing him. "So, you and the man you went out with tonight."

"Humphrey."

Even his name sounded staid and bland. "He's the same one from Tempo, right?"

"Yes."

"And you're together?" It had taken all his willpower to push the last word out.

Her inhale was audible. "Pretty much."

"I don't see a ring."

That did make him sound like an arse, but he didn't care anymore.

"It's not official yet."

Those words sank his battleship along with all his fleet in the game. He'd lost her. Again.

Another soft snore from the baby tore through the quiet hanging between them, and it felt like his cue to get up and get lost. What else did he have waiting for him anymore except being the best father possible to Nour?

"I— I'm happy for you," he bit out before turning and heading for the door. On the threshold, he paused. "I'll make it right, Rio. I promise."

To her credit, she didn't say anything. She must know better than anyone how far and deep he had fucked up.

He found his shoes, then his coat near the door, and waited outside in the blistering cold for an Uber to pick him up and take him back to St James. Through the trip, his decision during the conversation with Rio anchored to his mind like a beacon.

He now knew what he had to do. Even if it didn't make him win Rio back, it didn't matter. It was a question of principle, of being true to the man he was inside and not to the persona of the prince he phoned in on most days.

His watch read just past four a.m. when he entered Nick's house. It would be around five-thirty in Barakat. Bilkiss would be up. A devout Muslim, she never missed her prayers, much more the first one of the day. Propping himself on the edge of the bed in the guest bedroom he occupied, he dialled her number for a video call. What he had to say to her would be better face to face, and the next best thing to in-person was this.

She answered on the second ring. He'd indeed caught her around prayer time, her head covering on and baring just the oval of her face.

"Zed." Her tone sounded surprised, even if her features remained poker-straight.

He should take the plunge and get it over with. Would save them both any suffering.

"I can't go ahead with the wedding, Bilkiss."

Finally, the words had been spoken aloud.

Her eyebrows rose as her nose scrunched up. "May I ask why?"

Whatever respect she had for him would go down

the drain with his following words, but she deserved the truth.

"I loved someone back in London, and I just found out we have a son." He paused for a deep breath. "I still love her, and I think we should see if we have a chance, her and me. For the baby."

Her silence rang heavy for long seconds. Then she took a deep breath and spoke.

"You should see if you have a chance for *you*, Zed. For you and her. Not just for the baby."

The strength and conviction in her tone stunned him. "You mean it?"

She smiled. "Love. It's the most beautiful thing in the world."

"But what about you?" He *was* leaving her in the lurch here. Yet, he couldn't do anything else.

"Don't worry about me." A trilling laugh escaped her, light and joyful. "You won't believe me when I tell you I just asked God to send me a sign not five minutes ago on the prayer mat."

"So this is a good thing?"

"Definitely a good thing," she chimed with another laugh. "What's her name?"

"Rio. Short for Riona."

"Pretty. And your son?"

"Nour."

She smiled. "It means bright light."

"It does," he concurred.

"I hope to meet them sometime."

"I'd like it." Bilkiss was a friend; she'd just proven that a thousand-fold.

"Be happy, Zed."

"You, too."

"*Allah hafiz*," she greeted before ending the call.

God knows best. Nothing could shake her faith, it seemed.

A gigantic sigh rolled out of him as he dropped the phone on the bed and let himself fall back on the mattress. So that had been taken care of. He should move on to the next item on the list.

Sitting back up, he grabbed the phone again, wondering if Dilmas might still be up at this hour of the morning.

CHAPTER SEVEN

RIO WAS fielding a call and trying unsuccessfully to find the appropriate invoice in the mass of papers on her desk. Where was Martha when she needed her? Over the past week, her super-efficient PA seemed to have vanished into thin air. What on Earth was going on? Things couldn't keep up this way. Not if she wanted to run this ship without it sinking.

She went out of the office with resolute steps, spotting Martha's handbag next to the empty chair at the PA's desk. Good—meant she was around. Rio finally found her in the Mess room with a cup of tea in her hands, her knuckles almost white around the ceramic handle. She paused on the threshold at the sight of the red and puffy face of the blonde.

"Is everything all right?" she asked.

Martha sniffled and nodded.

Seriously, though, something must have happened.

"Is your cat okay?"

A watery smile made itself known. "Bubbles is fine, thank you."

From what she knew of her PA, Martha didn't have anyone else but her precious Bubbles. Unless ... "Did someone break your heart?"

The wordless nod and the pinched lips as if to bite back a sob was all the answer she needed, and she moved into the room to wrap her arms around Martha.

"I'm sorry," she said when she pulled away. "I'd give you the day off if I could, but you know how much I need you right now."

Martha nodded again. "It's okay. It might sound masochist, but I actually prefer being here. And it's not like he ever knew I existed, you know."

She wanted to tell the woman that whoever the bloke was, he was an arse. But she didn't have this kind of BFF friendship with her employee, so she settled for a smile and a soft press of her shoulder.

Out of the corner of her eye, she caught sight of movement. She and Martha turned towards the opened doorway when a man stood.

"If you'll excuse me," Martha mumbled, then made her way out.

Zediah stepped aside to let her pass. All the while, Rio's eyes remained glued to him standing there. She hadn't seen him since early Saturday morning when she'd returned from the gala to find him still there and their son so miserable with yet another teething episode. Nine months was a bit early for such happenings, but some babies did seem to start cutting their teeth as early as eight months. Just their luck, Nour turned out precocious in this aspect.

The words Zediah had spoken then had stayed with her, though. He'd said he would make things right, but what did he imply? Would he really stay, turn his back on his family? Families were tricky often. One didn't get to choose, so they got saddled with whatever Fate had lumped them with. She should know. But it wasn't reason enough to forego them entirely. He'd already caved in once. Who said he wouldn't do it a second time?

"Rio. Hey."

His soft greeting pulled her from her musings, and she gave him a small smile in return.

"You got a minute for me?" He grimaced. "Well, an hour or two would be more like it."

She narrowed her eyes at him. Something seemed different. He'd dressed in a charcoal grey suit today, still the epitome of the successful businessman. But something rankled.

Was it in the way he stood, straighter but also like he wasn't forcing the pose?

Previously, a hint of discomfort shadowed him like he didn't really fit in but was doing his best.

That seemed to be gone today. His broad forehead had also lost the frown he perpetually carried, his eyes no longer with the hint of a squint to them. They actually seemed to sparkle? No, wait, those lines at the outer corners hadn't been there before. He was *smiling*? With his whole face?

"Do you?" he asked.

Another blink and she returned to the present. An hour or two? "Whatever for?"

"It's a surprise."

The genuine smile coming with those words looked cheeky and so carefree. A hand squeezed her heart at witnessing the change in his face. He'd been breathtaking before, but like this, he looked beautiful. She had no other word for it.

She threw a look at her watch. She still had so much work to do today, but the excitement brimming about him proved contagious and infected her, too. Would Martha be able to cope? She could always tell the staff to be on the lookout for a potential breakdown.

Zediah's bustling energy made her want to play hooky. "I have to be back in three hours for an important meeting."

Granted, it was Kelsey dropping by the place, but she was doing so as the foundation's chairperson, not as Rio's bestie.

"Ample time."

The smile grew more expansive, and the clench in her chest tightened. Why did he have to look so gorgeous? And more importantly, why did he have to make her wonder, even for just a second before she pushed the thought away, that things could've been great between them if they'd been given a chance?

If *he* had given them the chance.

This reflection sobered her elation. She took a deep breath and walked past Zediah on the way to her office. The heat radiating from his body threw her nerves haywire when her arm brushed against him. How was that even possible when she wore a long-sleeved cashmere jumper, and he had on a wool-blend suit?

This was dangerous, and she couldn't afford this. Not now. Shaking her head, she went into her office and grabbed her coat and bag. "I assume we're taking my car?"

He nodded. "Unless you want to Uber there."

"Where exactly is *there*?"

"It's a surprise," he said once more, his smile widening.

A huff escaped her. While she didn't hate surprises, she really disliked them.

"Will I be able to park?"

"Yep."

Okay, one less worry. She'd deal with whatever he lobbed her way when the time came.

She threw a quick look at Martha at her desk, busy typing on her keyboard. At least the tears seemed to have staved off. Passing by one of her senior-most teachers, she dropped a quick word with him telling him to keep an eye on her PA as she was going out for a few.

Zediah followed behind her. And once inside the Range Rover, she forced her mind to blip out the larger-than-life presence of the man beside her and followed his directions, taking them past Woodbury Down to ... Leyton? She frowned as they entered the multicultural residential hub of East London. What were they doing here? Aside from a few Mauritian relatives who lived there, she knew no one from the area.

In front of another row of Victorian terraced houses, which looked identical to ones on other streets around here, he told her to stop the car and got out. He walked over to her side and held the door for her as she exited.

After she'd pressed the key fob to secure the locks, he placed a hand softly at her elbow to guide her to the front door painted red. A gentle tingle raced up her arm from where he touched her, but she blipped it aside, wondering why they were here.

She didn't have long to wait. He pressed the doorbell, and the door swung open barely a second later as if the person inside had been waiting for them. Her mouth hung open when she saw who it was.

"Jalil?"

The youngster grinned wide and rushed out to wrap her in his arms. The air whooshed out of her as he grabbed her and held her tight, his body trembling, shaking. With sobs, she realized. That poor lad. She hugged him back, which made him tighten his arms around her as he all-out cried now.

Over his shoulder, she looked at Zediah and mouthed her concern.

He smiled and shook his head. She lost some of her apprehension and held on tight to the boy who sobbed in her embrace.

When Jalil finally pulled away, he quickly wiped his face with the sleeves of his hoodie and tugged hard on her hand.

"He did it, Rio."

She frowned again. "Who did what?"

"Rio! *Ukhti!*"

Only one person called her 'sister' this way. She looked up to find the vast form of Quraisha Khaleeji, Jalil's mother, as usual, draped in a black abaya and a colourful scarf. The woman opened her arms from the hallway of the house.

With a smile, she went gladly and let herself be smothered against the ample bosom. Amid a flurry of English mingled with Arabic, Quraisha grabbed Rio's hand and tugged her farther inside the house. Rio found herself in a cosy front room with Arabic calligraphy displayed prominently on the walls. She sat on a squishy sofa, a cup of mint tea thrust into her hand.

What on Earth was going on here? She glanced sideways to Zediah, who simply shrugged, even though the soft smile never left his face. A pang hit her heart at witnessing that. Still, the rapid-fire squealing and talking around her shunted her back into a haze from which she managed to pick up the most significant bits and pieces of the narrative.

Turned out Zediah had gone looking for Jalil, finding the lad and his mother in the dangerous estate where they lived. He had moved them to this house in this safe neighbourhood and had extended a production contract to the young artist.

A lump settled in her throat as she watched the joy around her. She had seen this family at their lowest. When Jalil had failed his exams, Quraisha's world had almost come tumbling down. The woman had done her best to keep her son from falling into the clutches of the gangs prowling the area.

The last time Rio had come to see them, Jalil had angrily told her to leave. That had stung, but she hadn't taken it to heart, knowing the boy hurt. Because he'd been let down. Instead, she'd redirected her anger to Switz Bagumi for all of seven seconds. What good would it have brought to dwell on this disappointment even longer? She'd moved on, trying to help Quraisha where she could.

Her gaze slid to Zediah. He had come back, and he had delivered. Over a year later, but not too late, it seemed.

Could the same be said about their relationship?

She didn't get a chance to ponder this question more that day. Jalil wanted her to listen to the first track he was working on with Dilmas. For this, they all had to go to the studio located near Highbury in North London.

Another shock awaited her there, whereby she found out the name of Switz Bagumi's record label. RioLight Productions. He'd named it after her, and unknowingly, after Nour, too.

By this point, it was time for her to get back to her meeting with Kelsey, so she left them there and returned to Camden, thoughts and 'what ifs' swirling in her head.

Yet, she put a stop to those reflections. Where would they lead her today? Absolutely nowhere, so best she tore herself away from all of it.

As for Zediah—out of sight, out of mind for the rest of the week. She breathed a sigh of relief. He'd been spending most of his time at the studio lately, as she'd just found out, arranging with Oksana to see Nour during the day when Rio was at work. Suited her just fine. It was good to see him involved in something other than being a ghost haunting her house at all hours, plus she had her own life to live.

Friday night came and found her sitting at the dining nook in her kitchen when the doorbell rang. Oksana was upstairs giving Nour a bath before bedtime, and Rio would go up to tuck him in afterwards. This meant she would have to answer.

When she opened the door, the breath hitched in

her throat. Zediah stood there, but at the same time, it looked like an entirely different man. One who stood straighter, looking taller than his usual six-foot-one and leaner, more lethal in an ink-blue suit and black coat.

Yet, the wide smile on his face, and those quicksilver eyes that positively sparkled, softened the ruthless persona somewhat. Energy seemed to bristle from him. The kind that called to a person, infectious in the best way as it radiated joy and contentment.

She could even see it in the lay of his shoulders which seemed broader, in the smooth forehead now devoid of frown.

"Hey," he said. "Sorry, I'm so late. He's asleep already?"

Nour. He was here for their son.

Not for her.

She should remember it.

Opening the door wider, she smiled and bade him enter. "You can catch him just in time upstairs."

He could do the tucking in tonight, she reluctantly conceded.

Still in his coat, he thanked her, rushed past into the house and up to the first floor. She could imagine the baby happily squealing when he saw his father, the person around whom the stars and the moon now revolved. Nour adored him, and the feeling was mutual.

With a pang, she remembered the day Zediah had met his son for the first time and told her he loved the child already. She'd told him it had been the same for her—except the feeling had hit her from the very first time she'd heard his heartbeat from the sonogram machine and had then seen a little thing shaped like a shrimp inside her belly.

Zediah hadn't been there. He'd chosen to stay away from her. Had he known he would be a father, she had no doubt he would've been here.

But he hadn't even told her his real name.

She'd been a one-night stand to him and should remember it, as well.

And speaking of the devil, there he was, ambling into the front reception room. He paused at the kitchen's edge, eyes growing big when he saw the array of food on the kitchen island and on the table in front of her.

Zediah would always have a place in Nour's life, and consequently, in hers, too. She should stop rehashing what might have been and instead look to the future. One that would inevitably have him in it now.

She nodded towards the table. "Come. Join me for dinner."

He frowned. "You sure?"

"You think I can eat all this?" She cocked an eyebrow up.

"Why'd you order so much food then?" he asked with a laugh.

A sigh left her. "I didn't. My brother dropped all this off thirty minutes ago."

"Well, then, if you need my help."

She smiled when he removed the coat and placed it on the pegs in the front hallway. He also returned with his suit jacket off, busy rolling up his pale blue shirt sleeves before going to the tap to wash his hands. She averted her eyes from those strong, wiry forearms before wishing she could swap places with the towel wiping them dry.

"Grab a plate and cutlery on your way," she said, busying herself with opening the many Tupperware boxes in front of her.

Zediah plopped down on the booth across from her. "Is your brother trying to force-feed you or something?"

She groaned. "My mother, more like."

His eyebrows raised in question.

"My family owns *The Jolly Maharajah* in Southall.

The kitchen is catering for a big wedding tonight, so my mum made sure to pack a little of everything and had my brother drop it over."

"This is her definition of little?"

She chuckled. "Traditional mother."

"Eager to force-feed."

They both erupted in laughter.

"Shouldn't you keep some for Oksana?" he asked.

"She can't do spicy. She had a few spoonsful of the biryani, but it's her limit."

Zediah eyed the fare before them with a pointed look that he then directed onto her.

"Are you putting me to the test here?"

His question made her squirm further, but she steeled her spine and threw her shoulders back. "Are you a lightweight with heat?"

The flare in his eyes made her want to purse her lips. When he reached for the paneer korma, she bit back a smile instead. Game on.

He munched through a serving of korma, a plate of biryani where he mainly ate the rice, another serving of lamb madras, and almost the entire container of chicken vindaloo. He was certainly not a lightweight with heat.

She laughed and threw her head back as she settled against the booth, a bottle of Guinness in her hand.

"Told you," he said with a soft smile as he mimicked her, then brought his beer to his lips.

The same lips which had brought her much pleasure the night Nour had been conceived.

Focusing anywhere but on his luscious mouth, she let her gaze roam over him, noticing once again the lack of long locs.

"Why did you cut your hair?" she asked.

He shrugged. "Just didn't seem to fit any longer. I mean, I was back home, where family duties awaited me. It was a fresh start. I wasn't who I used to be anymore, you know."

She could understand him. She was lucky that she didn't live too close to her family to always have them on her back and could thus live her life as she wanted, dress sense included. If it were up to her mother, she'd be in kurtas and churidars all the time. She'd gotten berated often enough for not wearing a saree during religious ceremonies to know she should don some ethnic wear when going home for such events.

"Tell me about your family," she said. "It's a big one, isn't it?"

He nodded. "My father has seven kids, yeah."

Something in the sentence tickled her curiosity. "Not your mother?"

"My mother has three of the sons and one of the daughters. His second wife has the others."

At this, she blinked. "Is your family Muslim?"

"I wouldn't put it that way. Polygamy is more tradition where I come from."

"A tradition you subscribe to?" Her heart started hammering as she asked this.

He huffed. "One-woman man."

"Good." The word escaped before she could clamp her mouth shut.

He tipped the neck of the bottle her way as his eyes narrowed. "Because you're a one-man woman?"

"Not negotiable," she bit out.

"I know."

Made sense. He knew about Gary.

"Does Humphrey know this?" he continued.

Her stomach bottomed out. She hadn't thought of *him* in a while. He'd been away to see some sick great-aunt in the country. Out of sight, out of mind. She really knew how to do that well.

"He does," she replied, having caught herself. "But … it's not like that between us."

What had possessed her to say this? Next, she'd spill the beans about how she was moving into a marriage of convenience.

When Zediah didn't reply, she swallowed hard.

"He's giving me a good future, Switz." *I can count on him.* She didn't add this part aloud, though.

"It's been hard for you, hasn't it?"

She blinked at the question asked once again in his soft tone, the one that could blanket any quiet with its subtle notes that nevertheless reverberated so strongly.

"Who told you?"

"Oksana. But she wouldn't go into details."

The nanny, of course, knew all she'd been through since Nour's birth. It had been a stroke of luck that she had visited the Lighthaven shelter with Kelsey a few days before going into labour, and they'd stumbled upon Oksana.

The Russian girl had thought she would be coming to work as an au pair in Europe, but she'd been deceived and embroiled in a human sex trafficking ring. Thanks to the work of the Lighthaven Foundation, she had made it out of that Hell, looking for a second chance with nothing and no one waiting for her back in Russia. Oksana had been her rock during the past nine months.

Watching her son's father, who sat across from her, Rio wondered whether she should tell him what it had been like for her. It still smarted how he had left her in the lurch when he had returned home to Bagumi, and the small part of her still hurting from that pain worked itself to the forefront to spill from her lips.

"I had quite a few opportunities to get married since you left, since being single, and worse, a divorcee, is just not *done*. A few wanting a visa, but not as much as it would've been before. Brexit, you know. Then Nour was born, and it was apparent his father wasn't a White man, and certainly not Gary.

"I got the St John's Wood house in the divorce, and it fetched a pretty penny without even going on the market. I bought this place and settled here, even though my mother wanted me to rush to the cramped quarters they call home over the restaurant.

"There was a proposal from a rich older man in Surrey, with the caveat that I should leave my mixed-race baby with my family if I ever wanted to be his wife. Then there was this hotshot young doctor from Ilford. He wanted more kids as it would be his first marriage, and of course, my focus should be on his kids and not mine, so best I give up my baby while he was still so young and he wouldn't remember his mother."

The wince on his face turned into a look of pain, and his fingers tightened on the bottle in his grip. Seconds later, he put it down—it had really looked like he would've smashed the glass in his hold if he'd kept it there.

"I'm sorry." His heaving breaths punctuated the two words.

She shrugged, suddenly spent. Oksana, Kelsey, and Minnie, her sister-in-law, were the only ones who knew about these events. The ones who'd seen her cry when everyone else tried to make her ashamed for getting out of an abusive marriage and birthing a dark-skinned son.

She realized then she'd wanted Switz Bagumi to know about this, to understand what it had been like for her when he had thought only of himself on the day he'd turned his back on her.

"Humphrey had no conditions, I presume." His nostrils flared with those words.

"No."

"But you don't love him."

And it was relevant how? "Switz ..."

"Tell me you love him, Rio, and I'll be off your back. I promise."

She gulped. He would *not* play that card with her. She'd imagined a future with him once and look where it had brought her.

"It doesn't work that way," she said softly.

His lips drew to a tight line. "You once told me you wished I'd taken you away, Rio. Tell me again, and I'll do just that."

A sob hitched in her throat. How she remembered those words spilling from her lips, the hurt and the pain and the rage that had pushed them out of her to let them tumble onto him when she'd thought she'd found a safe abode in his embrace.

How she'd wished someone had taken her away from Gary before the abuse started. How she'd often wished this person would've been the gorgeous young man with long locs and fire burning in his eyes as she'd swiped his pint of Guinness from him to take a long sip. She might've been engaged back then, but it didn't mean she had turned blind and couldn't realize how delicious a man seemed when she laid her eyes on him.

But it was too late now ... wasn't it? He hoped his words would change what, exactly?

Shaking her head from weariness and a sudden feeling of defeat, Rio dropped her bottle on the table and propped her elbows on the surface, palming her face. After a deep breath, she lifted her head and stared at Zediah.

"What are you doing here, Switz?"

"I told you," he bit out. "Righting my wrongs."

He was indeed doing just that. Look at Jalil and Quraisha. Look at Nour.

What about her?

She didn't have an answer here, and he seemed to reckon the same thing. Slowly, he got up and started out of the kitchen. She felt too spent to follow him and to do what? This discussion would be going nowhere.

Seconds later, he came back in her sight, now decked in his jacket and coat. Energy pulsed from him again, but this time ruthless and sharp and meaning business.

"There's been only you for me, Rio. There will be only you."

With those words that left her absolutely felled with shock, he walked out of her house and closed the door softly behind him.

After everything that had recently happened, now this?

What was she supposed to do in the end?

CHAPTER EIGHT

THE NEXT twelve-plus hours happened in a daze for Rio as she tried to come to terms with Zediah's parting words.

It was Saturday, and she was looking forward to some quiet time at home while Oksana took Nour to Storytime at a nearby bookstore. Then the usual baby playdate with the other nannies and mums afterwards. It always helped to have a peaceful afternoon when she would then have her son entirely on her own for the night and the next day as the nanny would be off duty.

Alas, peace was not to be hers as a notification chimed on her phone.

Wedding dress shopping @ Southall

A groan escaped her. Of course, they counted on her to pick up the bill at the many designer shops they would be visiting. At least, it wasn't going to be at the mecca of all Indian high-end fashion in Brentwood, where even a millionaire would wince at the tab.

She had no way out, and with another moan, she remembered the many Tupperware boxes on the drying rack in her kitchen downstairs. She wouldn't put it past her mother to have sent all this food just so Rio would have to, at some point, come return the containers to the family home.

But this could prove to be a good distraction from

her worries. Or not. So, with a sigh of resignation, she got up, changed into wide palazzo trousers with her thermals underneath and threw on a long silk shirtdress on top. No way could her mother criticize this attire. Or go on a rant about Rio thinking herself above her station and getting all Westernized now with tight flesh-revealing clothing.

She was already feeling defeated as she left Knightsbridge. Nothing good could come from this outing, but what could she do? Unless she wanted to go on a pissed-off rant and scream the whole truth and nothing but at her parent, and then expect the sky to come crashing down on her head, there she'd remain between a rock and a hard place.

"Where's my Roshan?" her mother bleated out when Rio walked into the flat above the restaurant empty-handed.

You'd think someone had ripped her heart out with the theatrics. Rio almost expected the sound of a thunderbolt and then the view panning in and out on the older woman's face, three four five times in rapid succession. Then a high-pitched "*Nahiin!*" would fall out of her thin lips while she clutched her face with her hands in a very vivid rendition of Edvard Munch's *The Scream* saying 'No!'

Blast, it felt way too much like stepping onto the set of a Zee TV or Star Plus Indian soap opera when she came here. The vibe just seemed to do it to her, turning her into a drama queen who had inherited the tendency from her very own mum—horror of all horrors.

"Nour has a play date today," she said.

"And it's more important than coming to see his *Nanima*?"

It grated on her every time her mother used the suffix with her designated title. Using -ma tended to imply *she* was the child's overarching mother, with Rio just being an unfortunate blip in the picture.

"You'll survive," she mumbled under her breath.

"What was that?"

"Rio! You're here!"

Saved by her sisters-in-law—Minnie and Tanya were coming down the stairs from the flat above. The two must have been hunkering away from the venomous tongue of their mother-in-law. She so understood them.

A flurry of cheek kisses and hugs ensued between the young women.

"Come on. We'll be late."

Trust her mother to speak up or work some drama whenever the spotlight turned away from her. Dutifully, the three of them followed behind as the older woman went straight for Rio's Range Rover on the curb.

The shops were just a fifteen-minute walk down The Broadway. Still, they'd have to take the car given how Hema Mittal would love to rub it in the face of everyone who saw them that her daughter owned and drove a luxury vehicle the queen used.

Rio took deep breaths all the way and luckily found a parking spot in front of the shopping centre as a vehicle exited right in front of them. They all got out, and Minnie squeezed her hand beside the car in a silent show of support. Rio squeezed back, making sure to tag around Tanya as the poor girl was still not immunized against the sting of the matriarch.

At the counter in one of the Indian wear emporiums, her mother straight out told the shop assistant they were there to look at bridal attire. Rio exchanged a look with Minnie. This meant the skirt would weigh at least forty pounds with all the embroidery on it, the *dupatta* shawl adding a further twenty to the load. Tanya's scalp would be burning after just an hour of wearing this, what with her short hair that couldn't be made into a sturdy bun.

"We're not going for red, are we, because, you know …"

And here we go. As horror-filled Rio, she also reminded herself she shouldn't have expected any less. Tanya and Rishabh were already sleeping together, meaning the young woman wasn't a virgin bride who would honour the precious colour.

"Oh, it's okay," Tanya replied with a laugh as if she hadn't even registered the barb. "Anushka Sharma wore the most beautiful soft pink lehenga for her wedding."

Indeed, the Bollywood queen had worn a pastel embroidered skirt and blouse combination for her wedding to a cricket legend.

"We'd have to find the right pink for you, though," Minnie quipped.

"If you'd allow me," the shop assistant said. "This beautiful maroon and gold would look so much better with your complexion."

Rio took a step back as the deliberations went on. Her mother always found fault with every item the saleswoman removed from the shelf in its plastic bag and opened out on the counter for them to peruse. Thank goodness she hadn't brought Nour—the potential for baby spit-up to end up on these precious garments gave her the heebie-jeebies.

Almost an hour later, her mother had vetoed every piece of clothing that had been presented to them. Rio made a silent note to book an appointment for Tanya at the designer wear mecca in Brentwood so the girl would get to choose her bridal attire in peace.

"*Hema-ji!*" came a strident call from the doorway.

Rio, Minnie, and Tanya all moaned softly upon glimpsing the temple's biggest busybody, Mrs Savitri Sinha, converging upon them.

Rio glanced at her mother, who seemed to have lit up after being called by the respectful suffix attached to her name. Everyone hearing them would surely figure out she was someone important.

A little girl was flitting about Mrs Sinha. "You know my granddaughter, don't you? Nitisha. She's my Tulsi's eldest."

"Of course, of course. Such a pretty girl," Rio's mother was saying.

"And this is your daughter and your *bahus*," the other woman continued. She fawned over said daughter and daughters-in-law to kiss their cheeks and squeeze their upper arms hard.

They were still wincing from the pain as Mrs Sinha turned back to Hema Mittal like whiplash and started discussing them as if they weren't present.

"Still no more grandchild, *Hema-ji*?"

"What can I tell you? My *godh* is still so empty of a new baby to cradle."

"Have faith, *Hema-ji*. Have faith. You know my Dev didn't become a father for so many years. And now, his wife is expecting their third. And my Tulsi is in the family way, too."

"Yes, yes, of course. God knows best." Did the woman's words sound pinched? "What about your Smita? She just finished university, didn't she? Not engaged yet?"

"Ah, you know those young, modern girls. All about her career, she is. She is interning at a very good law firm in The City. I told her she should nab a good prospect there, you know. Them mostly being lords and such."

Rio frowned as her mother's face paled. Everything inside her knew the woman's mind was flipping at lightning speed in her database to find a way to one-up her rival. A churning sensation started in her stomach; this meant nothing good.

Hema Mittal gave a trilling laugh that rang

absolutely false. "Lords, you say? My Riona is almost engaged to one. He's actually an earl, but we don't really care about all this. All that matters is he is a good boy, *hain na?*"

Wait, what? What did Humphrey have to do with this? Rio hadn't told her family anything about him. They didn't even know about the gala. They'd have shown her any pictures if they'd found something in the society pages, blowing the image to take centre-stage in the family living room.

Everything inside her wanted to lunge ahead to point out she was not engaged to Humphrey, and more importantly, the man owed her nothing.

A soft hand on her arm stopped her from jumping forward at the blatant showing off of her mother. Minnie knew the mind games her mother-in-law loved to play—she would definitely keep Rio in check.

Rio looked her way, and her sister-in-law gave a slight shake of her head. As if to dissuade her from blowing her top off in the crowded shop made even more jam-packed as the two older women were blocking the entrance and only exit.

"Mummy-ji," Minnie went on with a soft tone. "Pardon me for interrupting, but we should be heading home, shouldn't we? Papa will be expecting his tea."

"Of course, of course. Very sorry, Savitri. That man would be lost without me."

Mrs Sinha cackled and concurred, and Hema Mittal walked out of the shop with her head held high, surely since she had ended up with the scene-stealing statement in the encounter.

Fuming, Rio went to the car and waited until everyone had packed in, then she started towards the restaurant. So this was what it would come down to?

"That poor Savitri," her mother was going on. "A daughter who refuses to marry because we all know she never will. Too much playing sports when she was young, I tell you. Turned her into almost a man, and now she doesn't like men. Hmph. Then Tulsi ran away with this dark-skinned playboy who fancied himself a Kollywood movie star. Have you seen how dusky her little girl is? Such a shame, really. Their next child won't be any fairer, I can assure you."

Could she stop the car and bodily throw her mother out? All her life, she'd heard veiled barbs about skin colour, yet today must take the cake. The little girl in the shop, Nitisha, looked like she'd grow up to be the next Jourdan Dunn. And, of course, such a beautiful model wasn't considered pretty as she was dark-skinned.

Rio herself had always been told she wouldn't amount to much since she wasn't fair. Combined with everything she had going on in her life right now, something had to give. Especially with Zediah's return and the cryptic statement he'd left last evening. This couldn't keep on. The peacemaker in her had had it up to here now with smoothing rough edges.

She waited until they were all inside the family living room before she started.

"Ma, something you should know."

"Yes, *beti*. What is it?"

She took a deep breath. "Nour's father has returned to London."

"Oh." A hand went to the dupatta-covered chest, probably in anticipation of a heart attack or needing to fake one.

Rio gave a short laugh. "I'm not going to beat around the bush. You already know this, even if you choose to not acknowledge it. His father is a Black man. From Africa."

"*Hai rabba!*" A swoon looked like it would come on imminently. "How could you, Riona? How ... with a Zulu?"

140

To her mother, all Black people were Zulus. True enough, Zulus were the biggest and most well-known ethnic group of southern Africa, the only thing Hema Mittal had chosen to remember. But that meant little when one knew the diversity making up the entire continent.

"He's not a Zulu, Mum. He's from a country called Bagumi."

"It's the same thing. They're all Zulus."

If her mother had spat those words out, she wouldn't have been surprised. She'd always known her parent would have no respect for Switz and even less for Nour when the bigot would have to acknowledge the kid had Black blood in him. Her father, brothers, and their wives wouldn't tarnish her or her son with any brush except love. But her mother ...

"You can't let this *man* be a part of your life, Riona."

"He's Nour's father."

Rio turned to see her dad standing in the doorway to his study, obviously having heard the entire discussion. She'd known she'd have his support, and a part of her heart that had been slowly shrivelling and dying under her mother's scornful words came back to life and filled with blood again.

"Can you imagine what people will say? We are in England. She could have found any White man to fall for, and yet she chose a Zulu?"

Her father's face grew stern. "To Hell with what people will say, Hema."

"Maybe it's easy for you. You're hardly ever out of that damn study of yours, always hiding from the world." Red was creeping up the face that looked like it was on the brink of exploding. "No daughter of mine is going to be with a Zulu!"

Rio was opening her mouth to reply to her, but her

141

father beat her to the punch.

"Then she doesn't need to be your daughter. Not when she has all of us."

A sob settled hard in her throat, and try as she wanted, she couldn't swallow it down. Tears pricked her eyes to then fall unabashedly down her cheeks.

Her dad turned to her. "Where was he all this time?"

She sniffled and wiped her nose with the flat of her hand. "He didn't know about Nour."

"But he's ready to do the right thing now?"

"This is not happening—"

"This is none of your business, Hema," he snapped. "Riona. Is he?"

She nodded wordlessly. Zediah had said it last night, right?

Her father placed his hands on her shoulders, which made her look up into his face.

"And you feel you can give him a chance?"

Pausing for a moment, she probed her heart and her head for an answer. Yet, it also didn't take her more than a millisecond to know it. "Yes."

"Then I trust you know what you're doing," he said softly.

As tears flooded her vision, she threw herself into his arms. A loud huff resounded in the room, but she didn't bother to look at her mother, faffing away all indignant and with her pride scorned. Nothing mattered but the gentle yet steadfast acceptance of her father.

"I should get going," she mumbled as she tore herself away and wiped her eyes.

But as she stared at her dad standing there, feeling the trust and love he had for her irrespective of what she did or not, she knew something else would have to give. Let the sky come crashing down on her head afterwards—see if she cared anymore.

With resolute steps, Rio marched to the kitchen to find her mother. She stopped on the threshold as her gaze landed on the older woman who had so much spite in her dark eyes. A shiver almost coursed through her, from the venom, or from the fear of going up against her. Yet, she couldn't keep things on this uneven keel any longer.

"Ma, I am not marrying Humphrey or any other White man. Maybe I will end up with Nour's father, who is Black. I don't know." She steeled her spine as the face across soured and the thin lips pursed as if in disgust. "But I'm done pandering to your views how I am worth nothing if I'm not married, especially if it isn't to a White man. I'm my own person, whether you like it or not."

A huff came from her parent. "How can you—"

She'd had enough of those theatrics.

"I can, and I will, Ma. I'm sorry if you don't like it, but at the same time, sorry, not sorry. It's my life, and you've tried to control it for long enough." She narrowed her eyes and took another deep breath. "And one more thing. My son's name is Nour. Not Roshan. *Nour.* If you can't wrap your head around it, let me know when you can, and only then will you get to see him again. Plus, he's half-Black, African, Ma. Nothing's gonna change that. If you can't accept it, it's your loss. Not my son's. Not mine."

With this, she pivoted on her heel and stalked away from the kitchen, not bothering to see what response her mother would give. Rio had said her piece, and she was done with the passive-aggressive abuse.

Minnie and Tanya hugged her again, her father kissing her cheeks as she said goodbye. None of them seemed bothered by what she'd just let out or by the drama that would surely erupt from the kitchen as she left. Good on them.

Pausing on the stairs to think about what she'd said, it rankled a little how she'd come to such life-changing decisions in the heat of the moment as if she hadn't thought them through enough. Still, a part of her knew she was doing the right thing for all of them.

However, the time had come to put her life to rights. To stop hunkering in the shadows while living in fear. She sailed down the stairs and out of the packed restaurant to her car outside with lightened steps. Once in, she paused with her hands on the steering wheel.

She needed to find Zediah and have a talk with him. While she wanted to give him a chance, there were still so many shadows over their relationship. Only when they'd shone the light on all those dark corners would she be able to step forward with him.

She also wasn't going ahead with the marriage to Humphrey. Even if she ended up on her own afterwards, if Zediah didn't want to give the two of them a chance, she was now okay with it. Like she'd told her mother, she was her own person, with or without a man. Humphrey deserved due consideration, though. The sooner she handled this, the better.

A short text later, she started the car and eased into traffic, all while thinking about this dilemma. He would understand, wouldn't he? Nour was the most important in the deal.

Humphrey wouldn't begrudge her thinking of her son. Plus, he deserved so much more. He was such a lovely person and should know what love felt like, to have someone who all but worshipped him. Like—

Rio quickly eased her foot on the brake, preventing the car from piling into the one ahead in the traffic jam she hadn't seen coming.

Realization filled her. All the pieces of a puzzle fell into place.

How had she not seen all this? Had she *chosen* not

to see it? Now more than ever, she needed to let Humphrey go.

His text reply came in, confirming the meet.

Rio quickly shot another message out and then made her way to Hampstead Heath, nabbing a spot a few shops down from Delia's Café where she had asked him to meet her.

Three o'clock on the dot. She was right on time. Now to hope her plan would work.

She got out of the car, approached the darkened glass making up the front of the café, and pulled the door open. A quick glance around, and she spotted him at a table in the corner. She waved at him and motioned to the counter, going there to order two peppermint lattes. She strongly disliked the stuff, but she had a purpose in getting this.

"Hi," she greeted as she reached the table and dropped her handbag on one of the chairs.

Humphrey, always the gentleman, had stood upon her arrival, and she gave him a tight smile thanking the Universe for the fact that he wasn't touchy-huggy. She would feel even more like rubbish for ditching him if he had tried to kiss her. It had always been politeness between them, and this would help smooth things out. She hoped, anyway.

The barista called out her order, and she went to get the clear mugs, placing them on the table. Next, she sat down and took a deep breath. A quick glance outside showed her no one stood on the pavement. She should buckle up and do this.

She cleared her throat and looked up into his face.

"You know Zediah is Nour's father, right?"

He nodded.

"I ... I can't do this, Humphrey." Motion outside caught her attention, and she glanced up for a brief second then returned her focus to him. "I know we'd said we were in this together, but it was before he swanned back into my life." A groan escaped her. "God, I sound like a total bitch, don't I?"

"You love him?"

She bit her lip and nodded. "I don't know what's going to happen between him and me, but I have to give us a chance."

"And you don't want me to wait for you."

"Goodness, no! I would never!" The sight of the soft smile on his face let her know he was teasing, though, and she chuckled then reached for his hand. "You're a good man, Humphrey, and you shouldn't have to settle for just a companion. You deserve to know what love is, to fall in love, to be loved. In fact ..."

She let go of his hand and stood, indicating with a raised palm that he should wait there. Next, she dashed outside, finding Martha standing on the pavement. With the darkened glass, there was no way the woman would've seen them inside.

"Come with me."

Rio grabbed her hand and led her inside the café, making a beeline for the table Humphrey occupied. She'd told her PA to come here on her afternoon off, or she would be fired. Hard of her, but it all stemmed from good intentions.

Martha's footsteps stalled when she noticed who sat there. Still, Rio would have none of it and kept on tugging until they reached the table, and she pushed the blonde who seemed to have gone frozen into the chair she had just vacated.

"Humphrey, you know Martha, right?" she asked as she grabbed her bag from the other chair. "Well, guess what? Martha has been absolutely head-over-heels in love with you all this time, and she has been crying her little heart out for the past week ever since she found out we were together."

She turned to the woman. "We aren't together anymore, just so you know." Looking at them, she smiled. "You both deserve to know love, and Humphrey, I am sure there isn't a person on Earth who will adore you more than Martha here. Still, treat her right, or you'll answer to me. Okay, I'll let you two get on with it now."

They both appeared stunned, and she bit back a smile as she made her way out of the café. On the pavement, she stopped.

The realization had come to her in the car—Martha's misery. The way the woman always lit up when Humphrey visited. How she got his tea perfectly right every time, the many peeks at the door whenever he was supposed to come by as if hoping to catch the slightest glance of him and it would make her world right.

If that wasn't love, then Rio didn't know what was.

She'd given them a minute or so to get over their shock. Pushing the door open just enough so she could glimpse inside, she smiled at the sight greeting her. Martha still looked pink, though more flushed than red now. Humphrey was spooning the crushed peppermint candy and whipped cream on top of his latte onto her mug. It was a favourite drink for both of them, and the fact he was sharing something he loved? Yes, they'd be okay together.

With a light step and an even lighter heart, she went to her car and got in, making her way back home. And with every mile bringing her closer to Clabon Mews, a crushing weight settled inside her.

Rio still needed to have a talk with Zediah. Could there be a future for them? Though she'd determined she could stay single, she didn't know what she'd do if Zediah told her no.

But after what he'd said last night, he wouldn't,

right?

She made it to her place just in time to have a shower and change and then have Oksana hand over the baby before going out for her free evening.

Environmental protection start-up bloke named Glen had asked Oksana out for a second date to a music festival in Bath. The nanny had asked for special leave and wouldn't be back until late Monday now. The perfect time to have a heart to heart with Switz Bagumi.

Nour was refusing to take a nap, and after the hectic afternoon she'd had, she did not have it in her to aim for an instructive playtime moment with her son. Instead, Peppa Pig would have to do.

With the baby's propensity to just roll over or try to crawl somewhere now, it would be safest to put him on the plush rug on the floor rather than have him on the bed where a second's inattention could result in a tumble and possibly a concussion or worse.

The high-pitched voices from the television settled around her. Nour tried to coo along to the sounds, imitating Peppa's snort a tad too well.

Rio took a deep breath and sent out another text.

RIO: *Dinner tonight?*

That should do. She hesitated to add the ominous '*we need to talk*' at the end.

His reply came almost instantly.

SWITZ: *Pizza? My treat*

RIO: *No anchovies*

SWITZ: *Pepperoni?*

RIO: *Perfect*

She smiled as she sat there in the room, the sounds from the cartoon blanketing her. After a few episodes when Nour's attention seemed to be waning, she picked the baby up. She made her way downstairs to reheat a tub of puree and feed him for the evening. There might be a need for a bottle if he woke up in the middle of the night, but given how he hadn't napped, she kept her fingers crossed he'd spend the night sleeping.

For once, Nour complied, puree not ending up everywhere, and she didn't have a slick of it on her. A miracle. Giving him his bath was thus a breeze, and she'd tugged on his fleece onesie when the doorbell rang. A glimpse at the intercom screen in the corridor showed her Zediah standing on her doorstep with a big flat box in his hand.

She went down the stairs and deposited the baby in his comfy playpen in the reception room. Having just come from the bathtub, he might catch a cold if she had him in her arms when she opened the front door.

Zediah greeted her with a wide smile as she let him in. He'd worn the coat over a thick jumper and jeans today. A far cry from the suits, and at the same time, it struck her how different he appeared as he ditched the outer garment in the hallway. More poised in his own skin, if that made sense. As if he had come into himself.

Nour squealed and started to mumble away happily in his baby language when he saw his father. Zediah wasted no time reaching for him and cuddling him in his arms.

The sight of him standing there with his child tore her heart in two, and she gulped back the sob clogging her throat. This was where he belonged. Ideally, with her in the picture, his other arm around her. Could she make this happen?

The baby talk turned to soft whining.

"He's getting sleepy," she told Zediah. "Mind putting him to bed in the nursery? Oksana's got the night and tomorrow off."

"Sure," he said, beaming a smile her way. "Say goodnight to Mummy, Nour."

She went to them and pressed her cheek to Nour's. The baby hardly left his father's hold to come to her.

But she didn't mind. After a soft kiss to his forehead, she sent them up then busied herself with getting the pizza box to the main suite a couple of floors above.

From the two receivers of the baby monitor—she also brought Oksana's up when the nanny was away—she could hear Zediah softly singing the baby to sleep. She shook her head and chose to laugh when she recognized the tune from SpongeBob. Well, at least he wasn't singing the Teletubbies' intro. She shivered with dread at the thought.

When silence came from the monitor, she ambled to the landing and called Zediah up. He followed her with slow steps, and she turned to find him standing in the doorway as if hesitant to come in.

True enough, she had brought him to her bedroom. As overwrought as she felt, trying to be lady-like in her kitchen or front reception room would've required too much from her. The little she had left, she preferred to save for the much-needed conversation she needed to have with her baby's father.

Sitting down on the rug, she patted the space next to her, then nodded pointedly at the pizza box on a breakfast tray. She'd learned the hard way how difficult it was to remove a grease stain from a shag-pile rug. Well, actually from the berating her cleaning lady had subjected her to.

"There's soda in the mini-bar." She pointed to the small fridge by the console holding the 90" TV. They needed a clear head for tonight.

He settled down beside her and reached for the pizza box. She handed him a napkin, and they started eating. A moan almost tore out of her at her first bite. The trattoria on the corner did know how to do pizza.

Zediah observed her, and then it seemed he couldn't keep controlling himself and burst out laughing.

She threw a cushion at him. "What's so funny?"

"You," he replied. "So the way to your heart is pepperoni pizza?"

Try as she wanted, she couldn't resist smiling back. What could she say? She did have simple tastes where dates were concerned. And speaking of dates, and why she'd asked him here ...

"It's a start."

He nodded. "And the rest of it?"

"That, you'll have to find out."

Silence thrummed between them for a moment. He broke it with a strong inhale before speaking.

"You *want* me to find out?"

On her reply hitched every step of their future. He was giving her the opening she'd thought would be much harder to come by.

"Yes," she said softly.

Another sharp inhale from him. "What about Humphrey?"

"It's over between us." She winced a bit. "Not that there was much, to begin with. But I set him up with Martha. They seem to be doing okay."

His eyebrows raised. "Martha? Your PA?"

"She's had the hots for him all this time. I didn't realize it earlier." She paused, tilting her head to look at his reaction to what she'd say next. "Everyone deserves to know love."

"They do," he replied in his soft tone. "*We* do, too."

He was making it so easy for her! This had been meant to be, it seemed.

"Can we start again, you think?" she asked.

"Anytime."

The few seconds before the word had come out comforted her more than if he'd replied right away. He was thinking about this, too, not just jumping in impulsively.

"But, Zediah. No more secrets. Or half-truths. If we

do this, we go all in."

A cloud passed over his face, and a vice clamped around her heart. Why had he reacted that way when she'd said 'secrets'?

"Switz?" she whispered, apprehension getting the better of her with every second he didn't answer.

When he looked away from her, she recoiled into her body. Everything inside her wanted to run away to protect herself. What was he hiding? Maybe a wife back in Bagumi? How would she live with this?

But he'd told her he was a one-woman man. She should trust him enough to hear what he had to say.

"Rio," he said with a sigh. "There's something you don't know about me."

"Is it bad?" God, she sounded like a lovelorn teenager who believed the world was made of glitter and rainbows.

"Depends how you look at it."

The chuckle, however, alleviated some of her fears.

"I haven't told you my full name," he continued. "It's Zediah Akiina ... Saene."

Rio blinked upon hearing the last word. Disbelief flooded her and made her frown. This name ... It was like hearing Windsor-Mountbatten, or Grimaldi, or Linden—otherwise known as the surname of an illustrious royal family. The Saenes were the royals of Bagumi.

"You're a prince?" she blurted out.

He turned to her and nodded.

Wow. She had not been expecting this. And as far as she knew, given how she hardly paid heed to all those lists about eligible bachelors in the society magazines, none of the Bagumi princes were married. So, if it was the only skeleton in his closet, she was safe.

As a realization bubbled inside her, so did the laugh that tumbled out.

Zediah frowned. "What's so funny?"

Rio only laughed harder, and it took her a moment to regain her breath. "I just ditched an earl today ... for a prince! If my mother knew."

"But I'm not going back home, Rio." Zediah shrugged. "Dunno for how long I'll remain a prince when I tell them."

His words sobered her up, and she ambled closer to him to place a hand against his cheek that had the rasp of a five-o'clock bristle to it. Suddenly, his deciding to stay here to right his wrongs took on a whole new meaning. Not only would he be turning his back on his family, but he'd also be doing it on his king, on the crown. One didn't grow up in the UK and not know the importance of royalty and its weight on its members. Everyone got to see the struggles of William and Harry and their cousins.

"Are you sure you want to do this?" she asked.

"For you? I'd do anything."

Her heart broke, melted, and then formed itself back up as she gazed into his dark eyes with a hint of quicksilver darting over his irises.

"You're sure?" she asked again, needing to know.

"I love you, Rio."

The words she'd always wanted to hear, especially from him. She'd convinced herself they held no weight and she didn't need them, but how wrong she'd been. Hearing him say them—and most importantly *mean* them—settled her world to rights.

There was no going back. Only forward. Together.

His hand came up and settled on the back of hers, where she still cradled his cheek.

"I might not be a prince for much longer."

Something in those words slashed like a razorblade at her feelings, as if his status meant something to her. But rather than get angry, she chose to focus on the veiled hurt inside them, the lingering of dread in the backdrop.

"I'd love you even if you were a pauper," she replied.

A chuckle escaped him. "Well, I wouldn't exactly be destitute without the crown's backing."

Rio smiled. This was her Switz. The man who could make her smile and laugh, who always made her think of joy and all things light and bright. She'd loved him from the very first moment they had spoken. Today, she acknowledged it.

"Then kiss me," she whispered. "Prince or pauper or whoever you are."

"Just the man who loves you, Rio. Just that."

He bent forward to claim her lips, then took over to prove just how much he meant those words. Heat and fire surged inside her at the contact of his soft mouth against hers. Flames burst, but rather than burn, they lit her up and warmed her every cell from the inside, bringing fuel to them, bringing life.

Their kiss went on for what seemed like ages, and Rio revelled in it, loving the feel of his hands as they landed more firmly against her ribcage and dragged her flush against him. Her breasts smashed against his solid chest. The pain a delightful reminder of their passion, and she wrapped her legs around his waist, wanting, needing to be nearer, to make one with him.

He wasted no time standing up and taking her to the bed, where he deposited her. She used her thighs to clench harder around him and make him tumble on the fluffy covers right along with her.

Laughter bubbled out of both of them, and happiness permeated her, joy settling in her heart to radiate everywhere until it blanketed her in bliss. Lips and hands trailed over her jaw, her neck, the dip of her collarbone where her jumper had fallen off a shoulder.

She went along, opposing no resistance when he removed the garment from her. His breath hitched when he saw she hadn't worn any bra. Why bother when her puny A-cups looked like mere mosquito bites on her chest?

Yet, when he kissed her there and placed his palms over her breasts, they didn't feel insignificant any longer. Because this gorgeous, virile man had been brought to his knees by them and seemed to think he needed to worship them, with his thumbs, his lips, his tongue.

Pleasure spiralled as she gave in and pushed against him, yearning, craving for his mouth to close tighter on the puckered nipple it sucked on. Trails of fire licked at the skin of her stomach when he tracked his fingertips over them as they went on their merry way to discard her trousers and underwear.

There, too, she didn't resist and play coy, just letting him divest her of her clothes so she'd be naked before him, finally. So he could keep on worshipping her like he seemed so intent on.

Hands and lips and tongue, all over her skin, teasing her belly button, then going lower and lower still. He kissed her the heart of her femininity and made her writhe on the cool covers that now burned her sensitized skin.

Her back arched off the bed. A plaintive moan tore from her when he settled against her clit and stayed there, bringing her to the brink. Then a climax came, rolling over her in waves, in ebbs and flows, taking and then putting back what it had robbed.

Through the pleasure-drugged turmoil, Rio didn't know how she managed to tug him to her. She kissed him, tasting her culmination on his lips, rejoicing in the almost-mournful groan rolling from his rumbling chest. She was now the one who took as he gave willingly.

When he tore his mouth from hers, she wanted to scream. Except he turned the emotion behind it from frustration to yearning as his long fingers found her core again and started teasing.

Just when she thought she would swear and tell him she couldn't take it anymore, he stopped, his sheathed cock now taking the place of his hand, pushing against her, into her.

She moaned and went against him, letting him fill her, complete her, like the time he had made her whole in more ways than one so long ago.

Their bodies aligned, found a rhythm as their skin slicked against one another's. Their mouths seeking a kiss that would bring fulfilment of another kind, making them one on a different level.

He drank the sigh from her lips when she came again, and she did the same for him a few seconds later when he pulsed hard and found his completion inside her.

Spent, he rolled them onto their sides, their foreheads pressed together.

"Forever," he said against her mouth.

"Always," she replied and kissed him again.

CHAPTER NINE

A SOFT sound tore Zediah out of sleep the following day. He'd actually woken up a little while ago, and turning over to watch Rio sleep would've been a tad creepy. So he'd stayed there, dozing along, content with the feel of her warm, muscled body spooning against his chest.

Pregnancy and a baby hadn't changed her figure much. The hips seemed a tad lusher, but otherwise, she was still the same woman he had made love to a year and a half earlier. Rio had always been a great dancer; it would stand to reason she'd work her way back to her pre-baby athletic self since that's just how she was.

The sound came again, like a tiny garble, high-pitched, borderline a squeal. With a frown, he gently extricated himself from the woman in the bed and sat up straighter, trying to find where the noise was coming from.

Always an early bird, he wasn't a stranger to sounds in the night. One of his first memories was of waking up in their beachside estate in Bordmer—with both 'r' pronounced hard and which meant 'coast' in Creole, the language spoken all over Bagumi—and creeping outside to watch the sunrise over the sea and listening to the symphony of birdsong at dawn.

This noise was no avian trill, though. One hardly

heard this in central London.

It seemed to originate from the other side of the mattress, on Rio's bedtable. He glimpsed the two baby monitor receivers there. When he listened carefully, he caught the mumble again.

Must be coming from Nour. Zediah threw a look towards the windows, then at the watch on his bedtable. Hardly daybreak, the sky still black outside, the patio furniture on the rooftop terrace the suite opened onto still swathed in darkness.

The baby seemed content to babble away. He threw a glance at Rio, still fast asleep. He should let her rest. After the night they'd had, she deserved it. On the other hand, he would have a hard time closing his eyes and welcoming oblivion again today. It seemed his internal clock was wired to the sun, whether the burning star proved visible or not. He should go attend to his son and let Rio get a much-deserved lie-in.

With an energizing inhale, he scooted off the bed and pulled some of his discarded clothes on. Feet bare, he padded to the door and went down the stairs to the nursery, from where the sounds were growing louder.

"Hey, little man," he greeted as he peered into the crib.

Nour stopped writhing for a few seconds, eyes wide and trained on Zediah's face. For a moment there, he expected the baby to start howling. The kid had always seen either Oksana or Rio upon waking. Even though they got along during the day, the sight of a strange man could come as a shock.

But then a happy gurgle fell out of that cupid bow mouth, and Nour started squirming even more as a big smile split his face in two.

Zediah smiled back even wider. Guess his boy was an early riser, too.

"Good morning, son."

Something lodged in his throat at saying this. He should have been greeting his child like this every morning for the past nine months. This should have been his routine, his ordinary life that was anything but, because he had Rio and Nour in it.

They'd lost so much time, but not anymore. From here on, these two would be his whole world.

The wriggling in the cot grew jerky, the baby language turning into a soft whine.

"It's okay, lad. Daddy's here," he cooed, gently lifting the baby from the bedding.

He frowned as he held the child. Nour wasn't this heavy usually. When he placed his hand under the little butt to keep him in place, he found the answer to the question. Soggy nappy. He should change it.

With Nour against his shoulder, he went to the changing table and made sure he had everything laid out. Even more imperative than in cooking was the importance of a mise en place with a baby involved. A second's inattention could prove disastrous.

Clean nappy, baby powder, rash cream, baby wipes—he had everything ready when he placed his son down on the plastic mat with cartoon characters on it. A hand flat on the baby's torso to make sure he stayed in place and didn't roll. He then proceeded to undo the sticky ties on the soiled nappy and remove it.

He pulled a wet wipe out with a deft flick of a hand and placed it on the exposed genitals. He'd been learning how to change the kid the first time, and as he'd turned around to ditch the dirty thing, a jet of wee had brushed his naked arm. Oksana had laughed and told him of the trick to always put a wipe or little towel on the boy in case this happened during a change.

He used another wet wipe to clean the area, wiped it dry with a soft towel, then dusted on powder when he found no hint of rash, and the clean nappy went on.

Granted, it took him three tries to get the sticky bits to hold just right, but hey, look—dry, happy baby cooing away.

A slight rumble broke the still air around them. Nour's stomach was growling. If he remembered correctly, Oksana had said his first meal of the morning was a bottle of formula with some cereal powder in it.

After picking the baby up again, Nour falling onto his shoulder to start biting, he scanned the room with his gaze. He found a few sterilised bottles already laid out on a table to the side, along with the tub of formula powder and the box of baby cereal.

How hard could it be to feed a baby? He'd seen Oksana do it. He could try. Thankfully, reading the instructions proved ingenious as every step was already laid out on there.

Placing Nour on the floor on his playmat and with a teething toy in his grip, he returned to the table, his son still in his sights, to make a bottle and then warm it in the apparatus meant for just this purpose. He tested it on the inside of his wrist as he'd been taught by the nanny, finding the formula lukewarm, so he decided to try his luck.

Scooping the baby up again, he then parked himself in the high-backed sofa near the window and cradled the boy in the crook of his elbow. Nour seemed to recognise the bottle and eagerly welcomed it, settling back to guzzle it down greedily.

Zediah laughed. "Steady, son."

Son. He got to say the word. His heart squeezed as he wondered if he would get the chance to say it for the rest of his life. And why not 'daughter' at some point, too? Did Rio want more kids?

The bottle over, he knew he should burp the baby now. Yes, he'd been paying attention to everything Oksana had done and said during the past week when he'd been haunting Rio's house during daylight hours. He'd always been a quick learner.

The burp came, along with a wet feeling across his shoulder. A groan escaped him. Spit-up. Just perfect. At the same time, a loud 'prooot!' tore through the air, and he would swear Nour's nappy just ballooned up in his palm where he held him.

"Nour. Man!"

With a sigh, he got up and went back to the changing table. A hand once again on the tiny torso, he proceeded to remove his own soiled T-shirt first. Great. He smelled of vomit now. He rubbed at his shoulder using a wet wipe and hoped the little napkin would do its job. Next came changing the baby. If he'd thought vomit smelled awful, well, that morning poo rivalled it tit for tat.

It was warm in the nursery. He could get away with not needing a shirt. Playtime seemed like a good idea to occupy his son. He doubted TV would be allowed this early.

So, there he sat on the mat, watching his baby trying to crawl.

Nour attacked defenceless stuffed animals, started raucous music by pressing different buttons on the spinning carousel. Of course, there was the creepy clown that lit up, the little piano making a cat sing along to the tune. It sounded more like the said cat was being eviscerated, but hey, he was no Simon Cowell.

The crying started an hour later, though Zediah had a feeling it had been more of eternity already. He loved this kid, adored him even, but how the hell did people do this day in, day out, and not go absolutely crazy? The reason for the howls was yet again a heavy nappy.

As he stood at the changing table switching on another clean one, he sighed and wondered how something so small could dirty so much stuff in such little time. And parents must go through those diaper packs by the hour, like a box of tissues when one had a cold. How much did children end up costing in the end?

Sunrise had hardly broken through the gloom of London by this point. Still too early for the TV, right? He sighed. He'd have to find something to occupy his son. Running to Rio and waking her up in a panic was not an option. He wanted her—needed her—to trust him, and he just could *not* crumble at the first sign of duress. He was made of sterner stuff than that.

Wasn't he? A glance at the exuberant little thing wriggling like a worm on Duracell batteries had him questioning himself. Nour chose this moment to look up at him and then burst into joyous laughter.

Fine. Baby 1. Dad 0. He had a new respect for parents with every passing minute.

An idea surfaced then, and he smiled. If it didn't work, he didn't know what would. Best he did not think of *that* for the moment.

Baby on his hip, he went downstairs to the entrance hallway where he had left his coat. In the inside pocket, his hand closed on the small tablet he'd stashed there. Now, where to go for excellent acoustics that, however, wouldn't shock the neighbours, or worse, wake Rio?

The cinema room on the lower ground floor sounded perfect.

But he should first make sure Rio didn't fall headfirst into a panic when she woke up and didn't see the baby in the nursery or anywhere on the upper floors. He went into the kitchen with soft steps, where he wrote a note about their location on a paper pad near the wall. Then he tore the sheet and placed it on her bedside table in the uppermost bedroom suite.

"Okay, Nour. It's us men against the world now," he said as they went back downstairs and then one level below.

The first door he opened was the wrong one since it led inside the home gym, where half of the space had been set up as a dance studio with polished wood floors and mirrors along a whole wall. Rio had surely had these put in after she'd bought the place given how most people would not need such a space in their houses.

She really had done well for herself and entirely on her own. Respect for her swelled in his chest, as did the love he had for her. She was exceptional. Phenomenal. And if she'd allow it, his.

Based on what had happened last night, he would say he was on the right track to make it happen, but he would never rest on his laurels. Rio deserved so much more than what he could ever give her, and for the rest of his life, he would happily pay this penance.

The next door proved the right one, the home cinema. The still air inside the room told him it was hardly used. Rio preferred to binge-watch things from her own bedroom, and Oksana loved to lose herself in a book rather than a movie screen, from what he'd gathered.

The plush grey velvet seats beckoned. After closing the door behind him, he made sure the air conditioning and thermostat were on the correct settings for Nour. He settled down in one of the soft couches that turned out to be individual recliners. Parking Nour on his lap, he powered on the tablet.

Greedy little fingers tried to wrangle the device from his grip. The baby looked like he'd start bawling out his frustration at being denied. Zediah thankfully managed to access the app he'd recently discovered and which allowed him to have a mixing table and digital synthesizer at his disposal right on one screen.

He set it to piano mode and hit the notes. Nour went still as the sounds erupted, attention rapt on the screen. Zediah kept on playing, and the baby began babbling as the strings started to resemble music.

When they'd gotten a rhythm going, Zediah added the synthesiser's controls on top, the notes now making different sounds that felt weird at first but merged into the other when the proper sequence happened.

They were hitting a false note when Nour lunged towards the tablet and slammed a hand on it. Immediately, the sound changed, suddenly harmonious.

A stunned Zediah peered down at his son. He'd been stuck on getting past this iffy tinge, his musical ear not able to work around it, and here this little bundle had seemed to instinctively know what to press to make it right. Okay, it had been more luck than anything, but there just might be a chance his son was gifted for music, too.

So he started a note, then played an off one on purpose next. Nour looked at him like he should quit fooling around. When he played the right sound, the child would squeal and try to hit the tablet again. Zediah let him a few times, their song finding a tune. Nour talked along in his baby language, and when Zediah laughed, he would laugh, too.

Then the mumbles coming from his son changed, becoming more distinct. Zediah paused and listened, and his heart hollowed out as he realized what he was hearing.

"Dada," Nour was saying while looking right up into his face with those big hazel-brown eyes.

Zediah blinked. "Yes, I'm your dad."

"Dada," the baby replied, as if adding a '*duh, that's exactly what I'm saying*' at the end.

This. This was his perfect life. He wouldn't let it slip from his grasp for anything. Not even his family. This place here, with these people, was where he belonged.

The events of the day all conspired to reinforce this for him. Rio waking up and coming down to find them in the cinema room, where they were still making music.

Feeding their son his puree, which ended up more like bombing the kitchen with the sludge than anything. Their walk, all three of them in Cadogan Square later in the afternoon.

Watching a SpongeBob movie in the main bedroom suite, all of them transfixed as the krabby patty formula got stolen. This turned Bikini Bottom into a post-apocalyptic, Mad Max-type landscape, and Oksana walking in right then.

"Sa!" Nour screamed in a happy greeting.

"What happened?" Rio asked. "You weren't supposed to be back until tomorrow."

Oksana flounced down on the rug and cuddled a wriggling Nour. "Glen is a pothead. And his feet stink!"

The rant went on, the movie kept on playing, the women in the room busy sympathizing with the other, Nour trying to eat someone's—anyone's—hair …

This was perfection. The ordinary made extraordinary because love tinged every molecule of the moment.

Zediah had indeed found his happy place here, now. No way would he ever relinquish it.

***

His phone rang on Thursday evening, from one of the few numbers he hadn't blocked. Nick had returned to the UK the previous Monday, and Zediah had moved out of his place the same day to come settle in the Clabon Mews residence. Had he forgotten something in his bestie's guest room?

"Hey, Nick," he answered with a smile on his face.

His best friend would no doubt rub it in his face how he had become pussy-whipped. But he knew Nick meant it in jest, that he was, in fact, happy for him, even though he had yet to meet Rio and Nour. They had something on the cards for the weekend, hopefully.

"Your twin's looking for you," Nick shot back without preamble.

All the blood inside Zediah's body froze, and he found just enough insight to remove himself from the recording studio and go into the hallway outside.

"What do you mean?"

"He called here, thought you were staying at my place. I didn't correct him. Be on the lookout, though."

"Okay. Thanks, mate."

He cut the call and pressed his back against the wood-panelled wall. He hadn't rung home since the past weekend. A quick text to Isha to let her know he was okay and would reach out when he could and she should not worry, but otherwise, radio silence with Bagumi.

His peace had lasted five days. Five meagre, paltry days. Damn it! Would there ever be any letting up from his family? Not unless he shook things up. And it's exactly what he planned to do.

He'd had perfect days here since Sunday. Waking up beside Rio after loving her last night. Getting to spend an hour with his son every morning before leaving for the studio and taking Jalil under his wing again felt like the most normal thing. He'd rediscovered his knack for making tracks. Then going back home to his woman and kid at night, to listen raptly to how their day had gone.

Was it too much to ask, to wish his life went on in such a steady stream?

After throwing quick goodbyes to the lot in the studio, he took a cab to Knightsbridge. He found Oksana feeding Nour his dinner in the kitchen. The lingering smell of vanilla and cookie dough told him it was the biscuity rusk the baby absolutely adored and ate without a fuss.

Guess kids the world over were born with a penchant for confectionary and an aversion to broccoli.

He still had a healthy dislike for the cruciferous, having no idea how—or better yet why—Rio chose to eat platefuls of the green stuff a few times a week.

He ditched his coat and had a chat with his son as the nanny cleared the kitchen.

The doorbell rang. He'd ordered pizza on the way over. He'd need all plus points on his side when he sat down with Rio and told her he needed to go back to Bagumi if only to clear the air with his family and make his position known.

It would break her heart to see him leaving again, but he'd promised himself he would be back by Sunday. Not a morning or afternoon would go by without him ringing her to give her a status update. Going forward, she would know everything happening in his life. He owed her that.

The early December air had turned frigid, and he wouldn't expose the baby to such temps. Come to think of it. It might be time to put another door inside the front hallway, turning the entrance into a sort of porch slash mudroom. The interior panel would keep the rest of the house toasty. Strange how Rio hadn't already thought of it.

He went to the front door with a few long steps and pulled it open and turned to stone.

His twin, Zareb, looked like he had a whole forest up his arse with the way he stood there stock-still. His dark eyes scanned the length of Zediah as if he were looking at something testing his patience.

"Brother," Zareb intoned.

Zediah took a deep, sharp inhale. "What are you doing here?"

Zareb shrugged. "No one was able to get in touch with you."

His eyebrows rose. "So they sent a search party? Namely, you?"

Another shrug in reply.

"What do you want?"

"You're needed back home."

Like hell he was. "Not happening."

A sigh tore through the air. "Zed, don't make this any harder than it already is."

He drew to his full height and crossed his arms in front of his chest. See if he would give in to this little mind game.

But then something else registered. Keeping the door open like this would drive the cold inside, and this could hurt Nour. And staying here to have an argument on the stoop just wasn't done—who knew if someone put the pieces together and realized they were two Bagumi princes having a heated tiff? It had been drilled inside all of them to avoid any kind of public exposure.

So Zediah found himself with no other choice but to invite his sibling inside. True, it was Rio's place and not his, but he'd pack up this inconvenience soon enough and have him on his un-merry way back to Bagumi.

Zareb had the decency to wait for him to close the door and start inside, following in his wake and not barging in already. The eyebrows on the other man's face rose when his gaze encountered Oksana standing there in the kitchen with Nour in her arms.

His brother would, however, know this was not his baby's mother. As head of palace security, there was truly little about family dealings Zareb didn't know about. Oksana was staring at him all agog, and Zediah sighed while he rolled his eyes. His brothers were always having this kind of effect on women.

"Zareb, this is Nour, my son, and Oksana, his nanny." He then turned to the young woman. "This is my brother."

The blonde blinked. "Wow, you two sure come from a fantastic gene pool."

Was a smile twitching at the corners of Zareb's lips?

Zediah nodded at the baby. "Would you mind ...?"

"Oh." She seemed to snap out of a spell. "Sure. We'll be up in the nursery. Nour needs a bath, then it's bedtime."

The two men waited for her to leave before turning to face each other again.

Zareb waved to the lounge set in the room in front of the lit fireplace. "May I?"

"No." He would not make this easy for his twin.

An eyebrow cocked, but Zareb didn't protest.

"Why are you here?" Zediah again asked, his patience going a bit rough at the edges. Rio would be home any minute—he needed the man gone before she returned.

"Have you been living under a rock or what?"

"Or what," he quipped without humour.

Zareb sighed. "It's all over the palace, Zed."

"What is?" A sense of unease had been steadily building inside him, and the feeling had grown close to culmination now.

"Bilkiss."

He frowned upon hearing the name. "What's she been up to?"

Zareb gave a snort. "What *hasn't* she been up to, you mean. Yesterday, a security crew sweeping the Bordmer estate found her hiding inside one of the remote guest cottages."

"What would she be doing there?" This didn't make any sense.

"And that's not even the half of it. Turns out she'd been hiding in the cottage foremost on the beach since Tuesday after her father had a fatwa issued against her."

Zediah's mouth was hanging open by now. "A fatwa? Whatever for?"

Zareb sighed. "Officially for coming out as a lesbian,

and on the down-low for fomenting a rebellion against his government. Take your pick."

Bloody hell. Surprised didn't even start to cover his reaction to these two snippets of information.

Though the first one did make sense, somewhat— she had, after all, been terribly reluctant to set a date for their wedding. She'd mentioned on the phone she'd been waiting for a sign and cancelling the arranged marriage had been it. Made sense if she was gay and couldn't stomach being wedded to a man she couldn't ever love.

But the second bit had him shaking his head in disbelief. He was still reeling when the front door opened, and Rio came in. She stopped on the threshold of the main reception area, a puzzled expression on her face. Her gaze went from Zediah to Zareb and back again.

"Rio," he said as he straightened and went to her.

"Hey," she replied, her tone cautious. "Who's our visitor?"

It warmed his heart to hear her use 'our' and thus include him in. He reached her side and placed an arm around her shoulders. Drawing her close, he wanted to protect her from what would come next, from the very presence of his sibling, representing his family, in the room.

"This is Zareb," he told her. "My twin."

She glanced up at him with a frown. One would expect meeting the family would involve warmer greetings and possibly a shake of hands, if not a kiss to the cheek already. But none of that for them. She seemed to know this was not a social call. He could feel it in the way she tensed next to him.

"Lovely to meet you, Zareb," she said with a polite nod.

His brother returned the nod. "Likewise."

A man of a few words, except when he needed to

can it and not cause further mayhem.

"Zed, your betrothal will be announced this Saturday. The king and queen need you back home right away."

Like now. He simply did not know when and how to shut his trap, did he?

Against him, Rio went absolutely still. Her face took on a stricken expression, and then before he could do or say anything, she had mumbled her excuses and rushed away, up the stairs in a jog.

Zediah was left suddenly feeling cold and bereft. And amid all the ice, cold fury brewed, and he turned this all-consuming emotion onto his little brother.

"Seriously?" he spat. "That's how you had to play it?"

The soft shrug from Zareb further incensed him. But he had bigger fish to fry, namely calming Rio down and sorting out the truth for her.

"Just piss off, will you?" he threw at his twin before rushing up the stairs in Rio's wake.

He found her in the main bedroom, outside on the small terrace that must feel like a frozen tundra, what with this winter weather. She didn't even have a coat on.

"Rio," he called out. She didn't turn around. From the stiff set of her shoulders, he hoped she wasn't crying. "Babe, please come inside."

"Whatever for?" she muttered in reply.

His insides crushed onto themselves. He did not like her defeated tone at all.

Reaching for her hand, he wrapped her cold digits in his palm and softly dragged her back inside, closing the sliding doors behind her. The tip of her nose had already gone red. He hoped it wasn't frostbite.

"Rio, listen to me."

A sigh tore out of her. "I thought we'd said the whole truth and nothing but, Switz. No more secrets."

"I have no secrets for you," he reassured her with his palms still trying to warm her cold hand. He reached for the other hand and rubbed it in his grip, too.

"You're engaged?"

Damn. He'd always known this would come back to bite him in the arse. "No. I was betrothed, though."

She blinked. "What's the difference?"

"Engaged is when you propose to someone." *Like I'm hoping and planning to do with you once we've hit cruising speed a bit more.* "Betrothed is when you're paired with someone in an arranged match."

Her mouth dropped open. "Royal families still resort to arranged matches? In this day and age?"

True enough, when one looked at William and Harry from England, Felipe of Spain, and Victoria and Carl Philip of Sweden, it would seem love always won over antiquated political dealings. Guess Bagumi had some catching up to do in that regard, though his sisters had started clearing the path already.

He took a deep breath and faced her.

"Listen to me. Her name is Bilkiss. She is the daughter of the president of neighbouring Barakat, and I broke it off with her on my first weekend here." When her eyes grew wide, he knew he should be more explicit. "There never was anything between us except for our families brokering this deal. That's exactly what it was, between our two governments without us even knowing about it until we were presented with the terms."

"You don't love her?"

Her voice sounded so small, it took everything he had inside him to not lunge forward and wrap her in his arms so she would feel in his embrace how much she meant to him—aka the world.

"I never have, and neither has she. Bilkiss is gay. And I told you there's always just been one woman for me, and it's you. Always you."

172

Her shoulders deflated, but his heart wanted to sing with victory and joy when she came up and plastered herself to him so he would hug her.

"Then what is this all about?" she asked, the words muffled against his jumper.

"Just utter nonsense I intend to remedy ASAP."

She tore herself away from him to look into his face. "You're going back?"

It felled him to see the depths of doubt and hurt in her eyes. Like the murky brown he had witnessed when her prick of an ex had been abusing her.

An idea suddenly dawned.

"Come with me," he told her.

"What?" She blinked, her lower lip trembling.

"Come with me to Bagumi. Let me show my family that I am with you, and nothing will make me change my mind. Whether they accept it or not, we'll be back here by this weekend, living our lives as we have been these past few days."

She swallowed hard. "Zediah ... Is it really a good idea, to antagonise them in the middle of a political crisis, as I assume this whole shebang is one?"

A smile tugged at his lips. "All the more reason for it. Let's show them who we are. Riodiah."

A laugh bubbled out of her. "Oksana came up with it, didn't she?"

"She did." He grew solemn and peered down into her face, tucking a lock of hair behind her ear. "What do you say?"

"That we go to Bagumi and face your family?"

He nodded. "Trust me."

CHAPTER TEN

TRUST HIM ... Was this the biggest mistake she would end up making?

Or would falling in love with the one man who could break her heart take the top spot?

A sense of unease had fallen over Rio as soon as she'd stepped foot inside her house that Thursday evening to find a man who looked remarkably like Zediah standing there with him.

She wouldn't have said it was his twin right away, not even with the long locs, but definitely a brother. And the way he stood, all straight and with rigid shoulders, had augured nothing good. Hell, even him being here had meant the lid would soon be slammed down on the few days of heaven she'd known with Zediah this past week.

Then was the news of his betrothal, which he'd assured her was not relevant. Still, it appeared to be on the cards back in Bagumi. Rollicking nausea had assailed her. When he'd told her of his ludicrous plan to go back and face them all together, she'd wanted to say no.

But a part of her had reckoned the two of them would have no hope of existing if he didn't settle the score with his family. She had received her father's and her brothers' blessing—Zediah deserved the same on his side, too.

So bottling up her dread, she had acquiesced, and the ball had started rolling. She had, however, been adamant they wait for Nour to wake up in the morning before setting out; his routine would be upended enough with this unexpected trip. Plus, they were going on a private plane, so they weren't tied by commercial schedules.

Zediah made her pack light, which brought some comfort—he wasn't planning an extended stay there. In, out, back here and going about their business as usual. She crossed her fingers it would all take place as such, and nothing untoward would land onto their path.

It took them seven hours from London to touch down in Bagumi, at the international airport located quite far from the capital, Darusa. She'd tamped down her awe when turning up at London City airport in the heart of the English capital. Planes were allowed only seven minutes on the runway for take-off or landing. Only the famous and ridiculously rich could afford to use this platform located next to towering skyscrapers.

The plane had been another jaw-dropping moment. This was royalty—of course, it would be nothing but the best for them. The height of luxury she'd seen had been when Gary had played in a World Cup for England, and the wives and girlfriends had accompanied the players in the first-class section of an Emirates A380 double-decker.

But even such luxury looked like a paltry three-stars compared to the lavishness of this private jet done in the softest, buttery leather and gold trimmings and where the food rivalled what would be served in a Michelin star restaurant. Veuve Clicquot champagne was offered upon boarding, but she declined, knowing she needed a clear head for what would come next.

To be honest, every minute into this trip did

nothing to alleviate the churning fear that had started building inside her. They were leaving London, her safe place. She was British, but what did it mean in Bagumi? Had the West African nation signed human rights charters and the like? Why hadn't she looked more into it before jumping the gun and blindingly believing Zediah's carefree words?

The Saenes were royals, the absolute law on the territory of Bagumi. Should they decide her son, who was a Saene by blood, better remain there with them, Rio would have no hope, let alone any means, of fighting them. No one in the legal world would go against a reigning monarch in a custody battle. It would be lost before it even started. They could take her child from her, and there would be nothing she could do about it.

But Zediah wouldn't allow this, surely. A quick glance at his tense face across from her alleviated some of her fears. He seemed livid, the fury inside him barely contained in the unyielding set of his shoulders and the rigidness of his forearms, visible as he'd removed his suit jacket and had rolled the sleeves of his shirt to his elbows.

He wouldn't let something like this happen to her and Nour, would he? The Saenes were his family, but still ...

His warm hand reached over and wrapped itself around hers, and she blinked up into his face. His eyes were hooded, the frown perpetually on his forehead now. He had looked so refreshed and happy this past week, his features all smoothed out, making him seem younger. There'd been a laughing sparkle to his eyes, a smile etched onto his lips at all times.

The press of his hand came at her solid, intentional like it wanted to be an anchor for her. Staring into his eyes, their quicksilver gleam lessened some of the stress on her heart, and she gave him a tight smile as she squeezed his hand back.

The captain announced they would be landing soon, and Zediah let go of her to buckle his seat belt again. She did the same, throwing a quick look at Oksana and Nour in his car seat across the aisle.

Zediah had been adamant the nanny came along, to not upend Nour's routine even more and give Rio a break as she would meet his family. Best the baby had all the safe landmarks they could keep in his life. His twin, Zareb, sat behind them, thankfully.

All too soon, they landed. Rio had not been expecting the shock to her system when the door opened, and she found herself standing there at the top. A gust of warm air engulfed her, her upper lip already breaking out in a sweat. She cast her gaze above to the partially covered sky, the clouds looking like they held a fair amount of rainwater in them.

Blast it. It was like stepping foot in Mauritius in the heart of summer when winter and probably snow blanketed London. Definitely a sudden change. Hopefully, none of them would get sick from the temperature difference. She should ditch the scarf she had wound around her neck, but the plain white blouse and dark blue skinny jeans outfit with ballet flats would look too ordinary without it. She would have to make do. Still, she undid the silk and then flipped it back on in a loose drape over her shoulders.

Zediah clasped her hand as soon as his feet touched the tarmac, and he helped her down the stairs. "Welcome to Bagumi."

She smiled at him, at the pride she could hear in his tone. He loved his country. It had been a good idea to let him come. She would never want for him to cut out a part of himself—which this land seemed to be—to stay with her.

A small sense of relief flooding in. She threaded

177

their fingers together, relishing it when he tightened his grip and tugged her along gently towards the convoy of Range Rover SUVs waiting for them.

Her heartbeat started galloping when she saw Oksana and Nour being directed to another car. They would not take her son from her!

With rapid steps, she went to them and put a stop to it, and thankfully, Zediah backed her up even under Zareb's frightful scowl. She would gladly tell him to piss off, though. No one came between her and her child.

The car seat ended up buckled in the middle between her and Zediah, the nanny taking the front passenger space next to the driver. Then the drive to the palace got underway.

Thinking of losing Nour in any way threw a blanket of unrest over her again. The churning sensation refused to leave her gut now, but she took deep breaths through her nose and tried to stave the panic off. They were in this together, she and Zediah, against the world. Or, in this case, his eminent family.

It took a while to get to the palace. She'd imagined Bagumi to be a tiny country like Mauritius, though there, too, it could take over an hour to get from one point to another. When the royal compound came into view, she actually lost her breath, her mouth dropping open in awe.

"Not too shabby," Zediah murmured next to her with a chuckle.

She cut him a glare. What an understatement. It didn't look precisely like European castles. Still, the sprawling buildings amid magnificent gardens looked like they had hidden interior courtyards all over, reminding her of the Maghreb palaces or even the sprawling *mahals* of the maharajahs in India.

The cars came to a stop in front of a set of massive stone steps. Strange, but no one stood there to greet them. Guess people. Namely they, came to royalty, and not the other way round. Rio made it to the top of the steps before a curvaceous figure sprinted out of the cavernous opened doors to the palace and headed straight to her to wrap her in lithe arms.

"Oh, I have been *so* eager to meet you!" the woman gushed.

"Isha, let her breathe," Zediah intoned behind her.

The woman released her, and Rio found herself looking into a beautiful face with a fetching smile and cheeks that looked like they'd been contoured by a master makeup artist. Except, she saw not a whit of product on those striking features.

"And this must be your son!" the woman, Isha, continued. "He is *so* cute!"

As Rio watched her approach the baby, she put two and two together. Isha was Zediah's older sister. She was also the one who had sent a boot up his arse so he would apologize to Rio after the way he had barged into her life. Rio owed her chocolate cake or wine.

"Damn, he's a little diva."

She turned to Zediah, who was looking at Nour, the baby seeming to lap up the attention being lavished onto him by his aunt. A chuckle escaped her. Nour had never really been shy. Guess he would take this trip in stride. Could the same be said about her?

"We should go in," Zareb spoke up. "The king and queens are waiting for us in the red reception room."

A cold shiver danced down her spine upon hearing these words. Zareb also had a borderline sinister manner to him, so serious and uptight, she could understand why Zediah said they were nothing alike. Did the man ever smile? No wonder he had become an Olympic fencing champion. He could aim for the kill with just a glare, no need for a sword.

The hand Zediah placed in the small of her back

eased up some of her nerves, but only just. Then he was leading her down a set of corridors that had her utterly confused and feeling lost after the fourth—or was it fifth?—turn.

Finally, seven-foot-tall, gilded doors were opened before them, and she glimpsed a lavish room done in. She had been expecting it, predominantly red and gold.

A distinguished gentleman with salt and pepper hair and a full beard stood near the far windows. King Ibrahim. Zediah's father. She recognised him from the few pictures of him she'd seen in society pages over the years.

To his right stood a tall, thin woman with walnut brown skin and locs of black hair with strands of white in them. Queen Zulekha, Zediah's mother. And to his left stood a darker-skinned, curvy woman who wore a glorious head wrap on her head. Queen Sapphire, the king's other wife.

Presentations were made, and in the haze of apprehension and nerves, Rio remembered how to put a foot back, daintily lower her knees, and bow her head in a curtsey to the king and queens, exactly like she'd learned for the waltz.

Zediah's other brothers were also there. Crown Prince Zawadi seemed like a man of few words, though he had a kind smile and the sort of face to make one think they could confide in him. On the other hand, Prince Azikiwe had laughing, twinkling eyes and the easy smile of a man who loved the good life. Didn't the tabloids say he was an ultimate playboy?

Of course, Nour totally stole the show. The royal family *oohed* and *aahed* over him. The proud grandparents peering down at him almost with tears in their eyes, and even the princes had goofy smiles on as they got to meet their nephew. Zediah was telling them all about his son's antics, and for a second, she almost convinced herself this trip here would be a walk in the park.

And then *she* walked in. The air inside Rio froze then erupted out of her in a gush that sounded like a plaintive sigh. She didn't need introductions to know this tall and gorgeous woman who could easily play an Amazon in a Wonder Woman movie was Bilkiss. Zediah's betrothed.

Queen Sapphire took the baby and approached Oksana. "Let me show you to your room, my dear. This little one looks like he will tucker out soon from all the excitement."

As the door closed behind their departing figures, a hush fell over the room.

Panic started going haywire in Rio. It suddenly felt like it was her against the world, against them all. They'd taken her son away. How she wished Zediah would come to her side and hold her—heck, even just take her hand.

But public displays of affection were a no-no in front of the monarch. So, he remained a couple feet away from her, a distance feeling as wide and cold as the English Channel. And all the while, her gaze kept returning to the absolutely stunning Bilkiss.

It didn't matter if the woman had said she was gay. She seemed to be opposing no resistance to being here, and a small part of Rio's heart shrivelled and died. She knew what was coming. The king said it a second later.

The best course of action for Bagumi, and Barakat, would be for this marriage to go along as planned. The fatwa was just a rumour for the time being. A wedding tomorrow, Saturday, would smooth it all out. Were they all on the same page?

It was an edict. She knew it, and so did everyone else. The silence blanketing the room drove the point home even more.

"Riona, my dear," the king was now saying. She shook herself to pay attention to his words. "It pains me to be doing this to you, but you must understand the tricky position our nation is in right now. Zediah has been betrothed to Bilkiss, and my other sons are also considering similar alliances. However, be aware, a second marriage is recognised under our laws. Zediah can still do the right thing by you."

A pin could drop, and you'd hear it.

Then Isha spoke. "Seriously? This what you're going to ask of them?"

"Isha," Zareb intoned with a warning.

A tiff broke between the siblings.

Rio forced herself out of the stupor those words had wrought onto her and lifted her gaze towards Zediah. He stood stock-still, his back ramrod-straight, and his eyes on Bilkiss, who seemed to cower there in the corner while looking pointedly at him.

Were they considering how they could make this work? How they could be together and stop the political crisis happening around them? They would make a beautiful couple, both of them so stunning and tall.

Suddenly, she couldn't breathe. The air seemed to get sucked into the vortex building before her eyes between Zediah and his intended.

Rio was never meant to be part of the full picture. Nour, yes. But not her. With a start, she remembered the first time Zediah had stepped foot inside her office just two weeks earlier. His focus had been on his son. He'd wanted a better life for the child.

He hadn't wanted a future with her at the time. Circumstances had pushed them together, their joining then inevitable. But what if those same circumstances had played out differently?

Eighteen months earlier, they had been at a similar crossroads. And Zediah had chosen his family over her.

Today, Nour was part of that family. But Rio wasn't.

The Saenes were the absolute authority over this land. Nour was a Saene, as was Zediah. They could demand her son stay here from now on. If Rio wanted to stick along, she could do so as the prince's second wife.

Officially, Bilkiss would be known as his 'real' wife, the one who would attend official events with him, who would be by his side in all photo ops and such, whose name would be on all the records as his legal spouse. She watched many Bollywood movies. The Mughal-era polygamous princes, as depicted in those films and in history books, took more than one wife. Yet, it was the first who was always the primary partner.

Mumbling her excuses, she took a few steps back, as protocol dictated when in front of a monarch. Then turned away and flew to the wide doors she flung open before dashing down the corridor.

Walls rushed past, opulent décor blipping through her peripheral vision. Though she lived in a rich man's zip code in Knightsbridge, it was nowhere close to this. The palace was a whole other world—hell, another universe entirely—and she didn't belong here.

A glimpse of sunshine caught her eye, and she forged ahead towards the French windows, pushing them open, emerging into a sun-drenched courtyard. The long scarf trailing behind her snagged on a rose bush, the soft fabric tugging her back and closing around her throat.

Rio came to an abrupt halt as she tried to undo the chokehold around her neck. The blue silk with the chequered jewel tones reminded her of a luxurious Indian dupatta. Unbidden, her thoughts went to another woman running desperately around the corridors of an empty palace, her beautiful dupatta soaring in the air behind her all while tears coursed down her cheeks.

Everyone who watched Indian movies knew of the

Bollywood classic tragedy *Devdas*. The titular character was a well-off young man who loved his poorer neighbour, Paro. When his parents mockingly turned her down for their son, her family married her off to a wealthy man, decades her senior, as his second wife. Upon his return and finding his love now lost to him, Devdas fell into the bottom of a bottle. Paro spent her days haunting the halls of her husband's castle, bawling her heart out for her lost love.

She might not have lost Zediah—she could still have him if she became his second wife. But her love might as well be lost. Like Paro, she'd been deemed unfit by his illustrious family, and now, she'd have to live the rest of her life with this knowledge scalding her bleeding heart like acid.

CHAPTER ELEVEN

"RIO!" ZEDIAH banged on the door. "Please talk to me."

When no sound except her muffled crying reached his ears, he slammed his fist on the panel again, this time in anger.

He should have run after her when she'd left the red room. But upon hearing his father's words, the anxiety attack he'd been keeping at bay ever since he'd set foot on the palatial grounds had gotten the better of him.

His vision had tunnelled and almost going black. He'd believed he would indeed lose consciousness this time as his tongue grew and wouldn't yield to any command, his lungs burning while his trachea closed.

He'd stood there frozen, rooted to the spot, unaware until the door panels slammed that someone had run from the room.

Rio. She'd heard his father's order and hadn't been able to take it.

Of course, she wouldn't. The man had been asking her to share her husband with another woman. Even if he and Bilkiss went into a marriage of convenience and never touched each other, Rio would still not be known as his first wife. She would be the other, second woman. Many still believed that of Queen Sapphire. And after what Gary had put her through, this would definitely have broken her.

The heated argument taking place in the room between Isha and his mother, Queen Zulekha, had brought him back to the moment as his breath had steadied. He'd managed to stave off the darkness closing in on him.

Getting his legs to work, though, had been a whole other matter. It had taken minutes to be able to tear his feet from the ground, minutes during which a battle with lines drawn in the sand with words had established itself around him.

"You can't expect them to go ahead with this farce," Isha was saying.

"It's for the greater good," the queen replied.

"My loves," the king said with raised hands to try and settle them down. "This is only for now if Zediah and Bilkiss, and Riona, accept it. In eighteen months, a quiet divorce can be ratified, and they all go their separate ways. By this time, the contentious points with Barakat would have been smoothed out."

"Seriously, Dad?" Isha's eyes were almost boggling out of her face.

Zediah threw a look at his brothers. Zareb seemed furious, and Zawadi and Zik had dark scowls on their faces. He was only just beginning to piece together the ramifications of the plan his father proposed.

Eighteen months? He knew Rio—she would never settle for being a second wife. Her man should be with her and her alone, in name, body, heart, and soul. He agreed entirely with this, too. Would she wait for him, though?

He'd put the crown before her once and look where it had brought them. A stroke of luck had made him discover he had a son, and he'd already missed her entire pregnancy and nine months of his child's life. In eighteen months, Nour would already be two years old. A toddler who would be walking and running everywhere, with an extensive vocabulary and the ability to kick a ball around with his dad, to make his opinions known when they made music together.

"I'm not spending all this time away from my son," he bit out.

Everyone turned to him as if they'd forgotten he still stood in their midst while they all discussed his life like he wasn't there.

"You don't have to," the queen replied. "He will be right here."

Anger rose inside him as he turned to her. "What about his mother?"

Queen Zulekha shrugged. "She can leave any time she wants if these terms don't suit her."

"They don't suit *me*," he said quietly.

Across the room, his brothers all straightened, their gazes panning onto him. Even Isha had gone mum and stared at him agog now.

What? What had he done to garner such shock?

"Zediah," his mother sighed. "This is not about you—"

"Damn right it is."

Silence descended on the room at the cold, quiet confidence that had rung in his tone.

Enough of this nonsense. This was the twenty-first century. It should be possible to settle political matters and territorial tiffs over a diplomatic table or some other trade agreement or charter. Arranged marriages should no longer be the only way to go. Maybe, as a last recourse, but had they even explored any other avenues of settling this dispute with Barakat? Hell no. It'd been expected he would meekly nod and step in as the groom on the day of this marriage slash political agreement.

There'd been a time when he would have. But not

anymore. Not after knowing he had a son with a woman he adored and who loved him in return and having seen first-hand what life with them in it could look like.

Never would he relinquish that.

Reckoning this made Zediah stand straighter and throw his shoulders back. He turned to his parents and steeled his spine.

"If she leaves, I'm going with her ... never to return again. I don't care if you disown me or publicly renege me as your son. None of it matters. Not if I don't have Rio and Nour."

"Zediah!" the queen gasped.

She would *not* play the blame game with him. His nostrils flared as he addressed her while his gaze still remained on the king. "Just how it's going to be, Mum."

Isha gasped, and Zawadi and Zik had wide eyes that looked like they would pop out of their heads at any second. Zareb, of course, just scowled harder.

"Father," he started. "Your Majesty. Rio is the woman I love, and I will do right by her and her only. I'm sorry if it feels like I'm letting the crown down, this family down. But it is what it is."

With bated breath, he—and the rest of the room—waited for the king's response.

A subtle nod came, no words. He hadn't won the war, but the monarch was letting this battle drop for now.

Zediah gave a sharp nod in reply, then after a slight bow, he turned on his heel and stormed out of the room and down the corridor. He needed to find Rio. She didn't know these grounds; she would easily get lost. The sooner he found her, the quicker they could grab their son and hightail it out of this forsaken place which seemed to have no care or concern for their love and happiness. On his son's head, he vowed they would never remain in any situation or location that afforded them this lack of consideration and respect.

One, two, three turns around this wing, and he still hadn't located her. Panic started to thrum in his chest as he turned yet another corner to find it deserted. By now, she could be anywhere, and he didn't have it in him to go look around the six-hundred-plus rooms in the palace and the fifty-or-so interior courtyards in its walls. He groaned, thinking of the extensive grounds which covered thousands of acres.

He was growing incredibly restless and desperate when a hand emerged from a sitting room and clasped his arm. He turned to find himself staring into the face of Mama Sapphire. With a groan, he lurched towards her, and she welcomed him in her warm embrace.

"Before you panic any more, I found her in the rose garden and took her to her room," the queen said.

He pulled away to look into her face. "She's okay?"

A dubious twist of her mouth gave him the reply he needed.

"Mama, we can't let this happen."

She placed a hand on his cheek. "I know, my dear boy."

Zediah took a deep breath. "I need to take her away from here."

"Good luck with that. Zareb still has all your passports, doesn't he?"

Bloody Zareb. Of course, he wouldn't relinquish the documents until Queen Zulekha said so.

He'd have to think of something. But first, he needed to see Rio. "Tell me where she is, please."

The queen nodded then directed him to where the guest rooms had been prepared for his arrival. They hadn't thought to put Rio and his son in his quarters instead of settling them and Oksana in the wing across the palace.

Rage boiled inside him. Honestly, this had gone on

for long enough.

As he stood in front of the said room and begged Rio to open to him, the feeling reinforced inside him. If he had to break down this damn panel to get to her, to go in there and pull her in his arms and never let go, he would do it. Then he'd take her away and never look back. His family had shown how much—or little—they thought of him. Leaving would be no significant loss for him.

If only Rio would deign to let him in, though. He could only imagine her hurt. Her heart must have been torn from her chest and trampled by the king and queen. She had every right to lick her wounds in a dark corner. Twilight was upon them by now, and not a flicker of light could be seen under the door.

Damn it! With another slam on the wood and accepting she wouldn't open, he sighed and pulled away.

"This is not over, Rio. I'll be back. And we'll leave."

How much did it hurt that she didn't even react to the last words? She must really believe he would choose his family over her. After all, he'd done it in the past.

The wall next to the door received a good kick. If only he had someone he could take all this fury out on ...

Zareb would be a satisfactory target.

As he started towards the main lounge wing of the palace, he gritted his teeth when a soft female voice called out his name at the other end of the guest wing. He turned to find Bilkiss in the doorway to her room.

Tired and overwrought, he didn't have it in him to be friendly or civil with her. After all, this whole mess got started thanks to her antics back in Barakat.

"Bilkiss, what the fuck?" he asked on a sigh.

She winced, then nodded towards her room. He followed her inside, waiting until she'd closed the door.

"I swear, Zed, this is not how it was supposed to happen."

He crossed his arms in front of his chest. "Then pray, tell how it was supposed to be."

She took a deep breath. "I guess you heard I'm gay."

He shrugged. "So?"

"You're not angry?"

"Why would I be? Surprised, yes, but angry?"

"Because being a homosexual is not what one is supposed to be."

The little hint of uncertainty in her tone calmed his ire some. "Bilkiss, one is not supposed to be a psychopath, or a serial killer, or an adulterer."

"It really doesn't bother you?"

He shrugged. "Why should it? Are you hurting yourself, or anyone else, by being gay?"

"No."

"Then there you have it. Full stop." He frowned as he stared at her. "But fomenting a coup against your father? This one leaves me baffled, I'll admit."

She sighed and flopped down on a sofa in the sitting room adjoining her bedroom. "Remember when you called me from London?"

Zediah went to the seat opposite her and sat down. "You mentioned me refusing to marry you was a sign."

She nodded. "A sign I should live my truth. And it's exactly what I did by coming out."

"Then?" It still didn't make sense.

"Then living my truth showed me how I should acknowledge every reality I had been shunning. Like the fact my father is an utter despot."

He closed his eyes for a second and exhaled. "There'd been rumours."

"Which I confirmed with my own two eyes. I couldn't let this keep on, Zed."

"So, what was your plan?"

"I'm leaving here on Sunday. *Angelos* is escorting

191

me to Avilar, where the king has granted me asylum."

Zediah had yet to meet the young king Gabriel of the island nation of Avilar in the Adriatic Sea. But the man's land had been under the tyrannical rule of a dictator who had usurped the throne for decades before the Linden family was able to win it back. It made sense his crown would stand behind freedom fighters who fought against a legitimate threat.

"I told Zareb this when he found me in one of your cottages in Bordmer."

Suddenly, Zediah sat up straighter. "Zareb? You were only hiding there until this coming Sunday, and my brother knows this?"

At her nod, fury boiled inside his veins. He jumped to his feet on his way to the door. He didn't let himself think until he made it to the lounge room where he expected to find everyone at this time of the evening.

Indeed, all his brothers were there with Isha and his sister India and her husband, King Omar of Sudar. The political skirmish with Bilkiss and his upcoming betrothal must have resulted in summons back to the castle. Isha's husband, Zain, couldn't leave his country too often as his people worked to rebuild Wanai after a despotic regime had been ousted. Sudar proved more peaceful, Omar thus able to accompany his wife today.

Courtesy and a healthy respect and abiding friendship between Zediah and his brother-in-law made him cool his heels for the time it took to greet the man. With clasped fists, opposite shoulders bumping as they each slapped the other on the back with their free hand. India wrapped him in a hug, then placed both palms on his face and asked him if he was okay.

He nodded, then extricating himself from her grip, turned to his twin.

"Zareb, you fucker!" he threw out.

Silence shrouded the room that looked like the

interior of a gentlemen's club minus the cigar smoke. A pair of eyebrows rose in question across from him.

"You knew!" he spat out. "You knew Bilkiss would only be here until Sunday. Yet, you had to come to the palace and blab about it to Dad and the queens."

"It was a matter of homeland security," Zareb had the gall to reply calmly.

Of course, the prick would play it this way.

"But what's done is done now, Zed," Zik said from the couch where he sat next to Zawadi. "How do we go forward from here?"

Thinking of the future slammed an anvil of uncertainty on Zediah, and all his bluster evaporated when he thought of Rio.

With a plop, he fell on a vacant sofa and put his head in his hands.

No one spoke for long moments, then someone did.

"You really love her, don't you?"

Zediah looked up to find Zawadi had asked the question. What good would it do to hide it? "With everything I've got and more."

"She's the one," Omar said softly.

Zediah simply nodded.

"You have to do something," Isha added.

He sighed. "What, though? Rio has locked herself in her room. The only thing she wants to do is leave this place and never look back, I'm sure."

"Has she told you so?" Zik asked.

Omar chuckled, and all attention turned onto him. "When you've found your person, you don't need them to tell you everything. You just know."

The tender look the Sudari monarch exchanged with his wife clamped a vice around Zediah's heart.

India had always seemed the most fragile of them all, and Omar protected her with his whole being. Yet, one could also see the man derived his very strength from this mutual love.

What about Amira, his sister stuck in the US while this drama played out? She would throw a tantrum for missing out, surely. She and her husband Jake looked like teenagers in the first flush of love, always giggling as they exchanged loaded glances that spoke a language of its own.

As for Isha, the woman had found her match in Zain Bassong, formerly a freedom fighter and now the president of Wanai. She went toe to toe, chest to chest, eye to eye with him, and Zain did the same since theirs was a joining of equals who shared respect and love for the other.

All of this, all of what they had, Zediah had found with Rio.

"I can't let her leave," he blurted out.

"Want me to tell the airport authorities to block her passport, so she cannot escape?"

Zediah turned sharply towards Zareb. For once, he didn't see any sarcasm on his brother's face. The man really meant what he'd said, offering an olive branch through the suggestion, even though it was hardly a good idea.

Something warm unfurled in his chest as he stared at his twin. Could this be the start of the mend in their fraught relationship? If Zareb, a stickler for rules and propriety, was extending a helping hand, it must mean he backed Zediah in this war.

"We have to do something irreversible," Isha said. "Something that will send a strong message but which also won't shed a bad light on the crown."

"What, though?" Zik asked.

Zediah was at a loss, too. How could they do something so monumental?

A sharp hiss came from Zawadi. "Rio is a Hindu, right?"

"Yeah, why?" Zediah was not following.

"Okay, stop it right there!" Zareb exclaimed. "I see where you're going with this. Zawadi, get out now. As Crown Prince, you're going to need plausible deniability."

His sisters' eyes had grown big, and even laid-back Omar had sat up straighter. Zawadi did indeed get up and walk out of the room, and all focus veered to Zareb then.

"It's simple," he said. Then he told them of the plan.

"Put them in front of a fait accompli," Isha said with a clap of her hands when he'd finished.

"But you're also going to need backup," Zik concurred. "A recording? Will it be enough?"

"Ooh, I know!" India smiled. "Live streaming."

"But not from an account with too big an audience," Zareb stated. "We don't need this to go viral before the king and queens find out."

"The focus on Instagram right now is on the charity's account, what with the gala happening in a few weeks," India said.

"Which would mean the House of Saene account hasn't been putting up too much content lately, and the algorithms won't pick it up quickly enough," Zik assured them.

Zediah had been looking from one sibling to the other as the discussion raged around him. It still felt surreal, like a dream in which his brothers and sisters were all rallying to his side.

Was it real?

"Guys?" he asked, then waited until they'd all turned to him. "We're really going to do this?"

Surprise further flooded him as Zareb was the one who stood first.

"We sure are," his twin said. "Come on, I'll take

you."

His sisters jumped up, too.

"Yes, go. We'll get everything ready. Grandma's Petit Trianon would be the perfect spot, don't you think?" Isha was saying as India nodded along.

Still, in a daze, Zediah found himself in the corridor. Zareb led the way to the side of the palace where all the cars were kept.

"Wait," he said, placing a hand on his twin's arm. "Why are you doing this?"

Zareb rolled his eyes. "To help you? Have you not noticed time is of the essence here?"

"Yeah, but you never help me."

The words were the cue to air all their dirty laundry out in the open.

Zareb sighed. "Have you ever needed help?"

At this, he shrugged. Had he?

"No, you haven't," his brother answered for him. "Zed, you've always been this guy who knew what he was about, what he stood for, and who wouldn't be afraid to tell anyone, even the king, to piss off if something didn't suit his code of conduct."

He blinked upon hearing this. "Really?"

"You never needed us, Zed. You had you, and it seemed to be enough for you. Believe me, we all wanted to be you when we were growing up, and Mum was pushing this or that on us. You always were able to stand your ground."

He frowned. "You sound like you're in awe of me."

He'd never have expected *that*!

Zareb shrugged. "Then you met Rio. And for her, you did actually tell the king to piss off."

"You're helping me because I went against our father?" This was getting a bit convoluted for him.

"Because you weren't afraid to do it. For her. She must mean everything to you, in this case."

196

A lump settled in his throat, and he nodded. Rio did indeed mean everything to him, along with Nour.

"So, are we going to do this or what?" Zareb asked as he started down the corridor.

Zediah smiled as a weight lifted off his chest and shoulders. A hug would definitely have ruined the moment. He'd be content with this new bridge-building between him and his twin. Plus, they also had a pressing matter to attend to.

***

Four hours later, they were back at the palace. Zediah had dropped by the side entrance of the guest wing while Zareb had gone on farther into the grounds. He needed to get Rio first, then grab a car from the garage and head out there.

The first part of the plan would prove tricky, though. Rio hadn't opened her door to him earlier; he doubted she would now. He could always get a master key from Zareb's office and sneak in, but he wanted her to trust him on this. For this, he had to talk to her.

Nour's bedtime was already past, so Oksana should have no trouble helping him out. Though loath to have to resort to such tactics, he, however, had no other choice. The least fuss they created in the palace, the better as they were on a clandestine mission here.

He knocked softly on the door next to Rio's room. It took a few tries before the panel opened partway, and a pair of suspicious blue eyes peered up at him.

"You're not getting him," the nanny told him as she started to close the door.

What? He blinked. He sifted through his mind as he blocked the panel, which ended up crushing his fingers. He yelped, then obliterating the pain, pushed his shoulder into the wood, and fully opened the door.

Oksana glared at him.

A lesser man would have shrunk in his shoes.

This young woman was an asset. Not only did she take care of their son brilliantly, but she also protected him with her own life. Loyalty like this was hard to come by.

"I'm not here to get him," he told her. "I need your help to get to *her*."

The blonde crossed her arms in front of her chest. "Why should I help you?"

He sighed, then told her about the plan already in motion. A small smile touched her lips, and she rushed to him to wrap him in a hug. When she released him, she motioned him towards the connecting door between her room and Rio's.

This one sure wouldn't be locked. At the same time, he couldn't barge in. But time was indeed of the essence here. He'd ask for forgiveness later. So with a soft click, he turned the knob and stepped over the threshold into her bedroom.

His heart stopped when he found her standing in front of the window, a pale wash of moonlight bathing her in its silvery glow. For a second, he remembered seeing her in a similar position when he had come down the stairs at her house to find her in the kitchen. That night, she had done so to give him an easy out.

Tonight, his heart told him, was no different.

Her shoulders had stooped, her back rounded; she had folded in on herself as if to protect her own heart. Her hair was up in the messy knot again, the locks tightening her face, and he couldn't dismiss the tear tracks on her cheeks when she turned to see why the door had opened.

Her eyes grew wide when she saw him there, and when she recoiled on herself, his gut tore in two and bled out.

"Rio," he blurted, then went to her.

"Don't ..."

198

He froze, thinking she meant for him to stop.

"Don't take him from me," she implored.

The word had come as the start of this statement which broke his heart in two. Reaching her, he placed his hands on her upper arms and clasped them gently.

"Never, Rio. Nour is ours."

"They won't let him leave, Switz. And I can't stay. Not when—"

Daggers slashed at his chest thanks to her dejected tone. Her hopelessness permeated everything.

"Listen to me. It's not going to happen. I am not marrying Bilkiss. Not tomorrow, not ever."

She lifted stricken eyes onto him, and he closed his for a brief second, avoiding the swirling brown of pain in their depths.

"But your family—"

"Sod my family," he bit out.

She blinked. "You can't ... you can't do this for me."

"Why not?"

She bit her lip. "But you're a prince."

"Wallis Simpson. The name ring any bells?"

True, he wasn't the future king, so he wouldn't be abdicating the throne for her like Edward VIII, but she must know what he meant.

"Zediah ..."

The hands left her shoulders to clasped her face. "Trust me."

Her lower lip trembled. "Promise?"

In reply, he leaned forward and kissed her. Damn, it had been hours since he'd last kissed her. Drinking the sigh from her lips reinvigorated him, the blood flowing in his body as it should once more, the vice around his heart and chest loosening up because that's what she did. She brought him back to life, made him the better man he always knew he could be, but not without her.

"Come with me," he said as he pulled away, then took her hand and led her to the door.

She opposed no resistance, and he stopped himself from imagining if it was from resignation or excitement. She hadn't sounded convinced he meant all he'd said. Well, what she'd soon see would speak for itself and for him.

With quiet steps, they made it back to the side entrance he had used. A Range Rover ambled there, and he found Zik at the wheel when he drew closer. He and Rio piled in, then the car took them inside palace grounds, towards the edifice of the Petit Trianon, which was a replica of Marie Antoinette's escape cottage. His grandmother had been obsessed with the French queen and had commissioned this structure to be built far from the principal residence.

Rio remained silent beside him throughout the trip, and thank goodness Zik didn't try to make small talk. Zediah nevertheless reached down and clasped her clammy hand with his. She didn't return the pressure, but it was okay. She would be convinced of his intentions soon enough.

Some twenty minutes later, they drew close.

Zediah's eyebrows rose when he spotted the small building. No wonder India was in charge of organizing the gala and other major receptions. The woman could turn any drab thing into a masterpiece.

Indeed, twinkling lights had been strung along the upper balcony and around the frames of the many windows. Undoubtedly poor Omar's job, as no one else was privy to this event. The Neoclassical style chateau with its dark sand-coloured façades shimmered in the night. Next to him, Rio sat straighter, and her hand tightened around his.

Zik stopped the car in front of the dwelling, and Zediah helped Rio out. As he closed the passenger door, something came into sight, and she went absolutely stock-still next to him.

To the left of the grounds stood a raised dais with four columns at the corners and a soft voile covering fluttering in the gentle breeze. A man in white sat cross-legged on it before a copper pot.

Zediah grew still as he watched Rio take in the scene and put two and two together. She had to know what this *mandap* setup meant. And the fact he'd brought her here ...

She blinked as she turned to him. "Switz?"

He gulped at the awe in her tone, the wide-eyed look, the mouth gaping open in surprise.

"It's for you," he managed to say around the lump in his throat. "All for you."

When she fell forward and wrapped her arms around him, he hugged her tightly and closed his eyes at the feel of her whole body pressing so willingly, so trustingly, against him. He'd managed to convey what he meant, and it was all that mattered.

Rio pulled away, stared into his eyes, then looked down on her attire of rumpled white blouse and jeans. "I can't get married in these."

He grinned. "All thought of."

Clasping her shoulders, he made her turn towards the trianon, where Isha, India, and another young woman waited.

"Go."

She seemed struck by shock, and it took a determined Isha to tug her along and disappear into the castle, where they would get her ready for the upcoming ceremony.

True enough, a Hindu religious wedding, the *saat phere* ritual of the seven turns around the sacred fire, wouldn't hold up in a court of law in Bagumi. But it was the meaning behind it that mattered. He wanted Rio as his wife and no one else.

This sacrament would bind them in the eyes of the divine, and his parents would have no other choice but to accept her as his one and only partner. The live feed on the House of Saene Instagram page would relay a blip of this ceremony, just enough to tickle international attention yet prove their joining as a fait accompli.

The idea had been Zawadi's until Zareb had sent the Crown Prince packing. His twin had then accompanied him into Darusa. He'd had no idea a small but thriving Indian diaspora existed in a sort of Little India on the west side of the town.

They'd found the priest at the only temple, the man sending them to a nearby shop where Zediah could buy the items symbolizing a woman had been wed. The owner of the shop, though, had probably thought herself inside a Bollywood romantic drama as she'd put two and two together. Then she'd pestered the princes how an Indian woman needed appropriate attire to get married.

Hence, their little trip had been extended another hour. He had gone cross-eyed looking at the intricately embroidered top and skirt combos called *lehengas*. Until the perfect one had tumbled onto the counter. The shop owner had sent her daughter along with the clothing to get Rio ready.

It seemed like ages later when Isha and India appeared in the doorway again. And when they moved aside, and Rio stepped into the soft light of the twinkling ropes all around the frame, Zediah lost his breath.

She radiated—he had no other word for it. The butterscotch gold silk of the outfit glowed with subtle warmth as its embroidery of pale-yellow glass beads reflected the light, the soft colour bringing out the rich tones in her brown skin. Her hair had been brushed straight, the large, embroidered shawl draped on top of her head, and light makeup made her skin sparkle. The dark kohl around her eyes brought out the hazel in them. The gold jewellery adorning her neck, ears, and arms made her look even more like a goddess incarnating as a human woman.

"Close your mouth, man. There might be flies," Zik said next to him.

Zediah shook himself out of his stupor and took a deep breath. He wanted nothing more than to drink in the sight of Rio, but they had more pressing matters to attend to. According to the priest, the auspicious hour for their wedding would soon be over. They better get a move on. To his relief, the old man, who had been adamant they consult the astral charts before embarking on this business, had discovered today was indeed the best day for their joining. It was as if Fate were smiling down on them.

When the priest looked his way, he took his cue to start towards the altar, carefully leaving his shoes near the steps. The mandap being a sacred place, no shoes should sully it. As he got on and took his place in one of the Louis XV seats brought out for him and his bride, the priest started with the prayers. If Zediah recalled right, this one was to the god Ganesh, asking for luck for the couple and their families.

His sisters then escorted Rio to the dais. He'd been told she would keep her eyes down and wouldn't not meet his gaze for this trip. The sacred fire was lit, and he looked up as a broad shape started up the stairs. What was Zareb doing here?

His twin made it to where they sat and crouched in front of Rio.

"I know we didn't start on the right foot, but I am here to present my sincerest apologies. You are good for my brother, and it is all that matters."

Zediah slid his gaze to Rio. A small smile had graced

her lips, and she nodded to Zareb.

"I know, sadly, your family is not present today," Zareb continued. "But if you will allow me? I've read your brother is supposed to give you three handfuls of rice to offer to the fire. May I?"

Rio nodded wordlessly as a tear rolled down her cheek. Damn it, his brother was making her cry! But it was true they'd had to jump into this wedding as a pre-emptive strike. She would have wanted her family present, and Zareb helping actually meant the world to him. His twin cared.

She hovered her hand, palm up, over the fire, and Zareb poured the rice through her fingers and into the flames.

Zareb left the altar, and the priest told them to stand. The shop owner's daughter, who had dressed Rio, had been roped as the unofficial helper. She gave them the flower garlands they were to place around the other's neck.

Rio went first, as tradition demanded it. Next, he took hold of the long necklace of gold and black beads called a *mangalsutra* and which every married woman wore, tying it around her neck. The long scarf he'd been told to wear over one shoulder was then knotted to one end of Rio's shawl.

The chanting started, and Rio seemed to know what to do. He followed along, fearful he would mess up. The Sanskrit words settled a soothing veil over the whole mandap and its surroundings. The flames of the fire burning harder as the priest dolloped spoons of clarified ghee into it from time to time.

He'd always believed this was the heart of a Hindu wedding—the seven circumambulations around the sacred fire which acted as a witness of their bond. He'd never known the meaning, and he doubted many did, but he'd had a crash course today.

The first round had the couple praying for food and nourishment. The second asked for strength on all levels in their life together. The third requested prosperity, all while the couple promised to stay faithful and respect each other. In the fourth, they made the promise to look after their family and elders.

Rio had been leading until now, the first four rounds concerned with family and household matters, which the bride slash wife would preside over. For the last three, the groom took the lead. Rio paused to let him step in front of her.

The fifth circling asked for the couple to be blessed with good children and make them good parents. In the sixth, they prayed for health and a peaceful future together. In the last, the seventh, they promised to live a life of love and friendship, with nothing and no one able to come between them. As the husband, it was now his duty to uphold these last three vows as the provider and protector.

And just like that, it was over. The priest gave them the blessing signifying they were man and wife. The proof came in the form of the red vermillion powder— the *sindoor*—between his index and thumb to then swipe a thick line of orange from Rio's hairline along her middle parting.

They were married.

"Kiss her!" Omar hollered from the garden.

Rio raised shy eyes to him, and he smiled as he leaned forward and pressed his lips to hers. Hoots and hollers erupted around them.

Zediah allowed joy to fill his heart. For as long as he lived, he would never forget this moment, the first time he had lain eyes on his wife.

But the shadow of why they were now married settled like a pall of doom over him, and threading his fingers with Rio's, he turned to Zareb.

"It's time."

His brother gave a solemn nod. The others also understood and sobered up. They would be going back to the palace and facing the king and queens. The woman and the priest were told to wait here, and a car would get them. The rest of them got into the three parked Range Rovers and made it to the palace.

"I can't believe you did this," Rio said next to him.

"I told you to trust me, remember?"

She nodded, a small smile touching her lips.

The return trip seemed to take half the time to get to the Petit Trianon.

India came out of a car and ambled up to them. "Part of the wedding where you were doing the rounds around the fire streamed directly to Instagram. Only a handful of views so far."

Zediah nodded. They should be in the clear with the king and queens.

Rio reached for his hand, and he clasped it tightly. One look and they started into the palace as one, a unit nobody would be able to break.

The throne room seemed ominous for this stand-off but also fitting. He and his wife—as well as his siblings—had gone against the crown today. Zareb had volunteered as tribute to bring the monarch to face them. They all waited with bated breath, not a whisper to be heard in the cavernous gilt-edged space.

The doors opened and revealed the straight-backed form of Queen Zulekha.

"What is the meaning of all this?" she asked.

In the past, he would have quaked in his shoes under the stern, scathing tone. But not today. Not when he had his wife radiating like an angel of redemption next to him. He tightened his grip around her fingers, and courage fuelled him when she squeezed back.

The king entered then, Queen Sapphire in his wake.

His eyebrows went up when his gaze landed on Riona. A man of the world, he should know what the colour in her hair parting meant.

"Zediah, what on Earth is going on?" his mother asked, her sharp voice grating with the incredulity he could clearly hear now. So she must have worked it out, too.

Taking a deep breath and gulping down hard, he stepped forward, tugging Rio along with him. She slid by his side under the prompt.

"Rio and I are married."

There, he'd said it.

Queen Zulekha sputtered as her face went red. His mother rarely displayed her state of mind. This must really have rankled her.

Good. She shouldn't have believed she got to steer his life as she wanted in the first place.

As she opened her mouth to speak again, a sound coming from the side stunned them all.

The king was laughing. Actual belly laughs. It even looked like he'd bend in two to hold his stomach in with his arms at some point.

Zediah exchanged a look with his siblings. By this point, Zawadi had joined them, as had Bilkiss. All seemed to be utterly shocked by the monarch's response.

When his mirth died down, he wiped his eyes as if tears had been forming there.

"Zediah," he boomed, then shook his head. "What else had we been expecting, though?"

Surprise still had all their vocal cords in its grip. The only one who seemed totally placid was Queen Sapphire, standing a step behind her husband.

The king took a few steps towards them. "You were always the one who never cowered."

With his father up close, Zediah took a deep breath and looked into the wizened face. "You're not angry?"

"I'm actually furious." Then he waved a hand in the air. "But what's the point?"

The older man then stepped to the side, reaching up to clasp Rio's face in his palms.

"My dear child, my son makes you happy?" When she replied yes, he nodded. "And you love him?"

"More than the world itself." The conviction in her tone rang crystal clear in the big room.

"Ah," the king said with a sigh. "Love. What are we to do when the heart takes the reins ... except honour it?"

It was what King Ibrahim had done with Queen Sapphire. They all knew it.

"Your Majesty, do we have your blessing?"

Surprise, then awe, then a boatload of respect flooded Zediah when Rio spoke and looked straight at the monarch, her back and shoulders straight as her fingers clasped tighter around his. This was his girl. She was back.

Another booming laugh resounded. "Call me Dad."

"Then bless us, *Papa-ji*."

Rio released his hand, and he understood why when she bent her knees, then lowered her torso to reach out, touching the king's feet with the tips of her right-hand fingers.

Queen Sapphire ambled up to her husband and murmured a few words in his ear.

The king then placed a gentle hand on Rio's head. "Bless you, my daughter. May you always remain a wife."

Rio seemed to find this blessing acceptable—he'd have to ask her about it later—and she rose to her full height. The king reached out with both hands and touched their heads. They had earned his acceptance.

As Zediah stood there looking at his beautiful wife, his heart soared as crystalline music built up in his soul.

Riona 'Rio' Mittal, soon to be Saene when they wed in front of the law. She had swept in and won him over with just a look, and she had gained the hearts of everyone present, too, with her radiant presence. Well, his mother would take some work, but it was a battle for another day. For now, he'd savour this victory.

Tomorrow, when their son woke up, they would be able to tell him his mum and dad were now married. Nour wouldn't understand, but it didn't matter. Nothing did, but the fact he and Rio would live the rest of their lives together, and Nour would always have his parents to love and support him.

Epilogue

Six months later ...

"I SWEAR this morning nappy must weigh ten pounds," Zediah whined aloud as he changed his son.

Strangely enough, no giggle came from the bathroom. He said this every time they gave Oksana a night off, and he woke up to attend to the now fifteen-month-old toddler on those mornings. Rio usually laughed. He frowned, wondering why the other side of the door was as silent as a tomb.

"Rio? Babe?"

He couldn't leave the squirming little worm to go check on her, though. By the time he'd donned the clean nappy on his extremely recalcitrant child who had developed an affinity for being a nudist, there had been a flush of the loo. Then the door had opened, Rio sailing out of it.

She came up to him, deftly wriggled Nour into a one-arm hold, and placed him in the playpen at the side of their bedroom. Then, she turned to Zediah, and the broad smile on her face alleviated some of his fears.

"What is it?" he asked. She had him on pins and needles now with this borderline beatific look on her face.

She smiled even more expansively, then took his hand and placed something on the open palm. He peered down to find a little plastic gadget, and— He frowned. Was this …? Looking closer, he saw two clear pink lines on the little window on the far end of the strip.

Blinking, he looked back up at her. "Is this …?"

She nodded, head bobbing rapidly. "We are pregnant!"

"We are?" he repeated like a dumb parrot until the realisation worked itself inside him. "We are!"

Laughter spilled out of him, and he took a step forward to wrap her in his arms and crush her to him. "Oh my God, I'm so happy. Rio, you just made me the happiest man in the world!"

She laughed, then pulled away just enough to kiss him. Seemed she had intended it to be a quick peck, but he took her mouth and sought a long, drawn-out kiss. He only tore himself away from her when something smashed into the side of his thigh, and a howl of pain travelled up his throat.

He glanced down to find Nour standing in the playpen, one hand on the edge, the other aiming to bang the wooden horse against his father's leg again. The kid did not like not being the centre of attention.

Reluctantly, he let his wife go from his embrace and bent to lift the baby in his arms, pointedly leaving the toy horse behind.

"How far along are you, do you know?"

She shrugged. "I suppose a few weeks, a month maybe. I'll know more when we see the doctor."

"We should go today." Any doctor in Bagumi would drop their schedule if the royal family requested a private visit.

"No can do," she replied over her shoulder as she breezed into the walk-in wardrobe. "I need to go check on the centre, then there's the opening of the care home on the outskirts of Darusa, and we need to be back by noon to make our flight to London."

He groaned. "So when will we see the doctor?"

"I'll arrange an appointment with my former ob-gyn in London, then she can liaise with the hospital here."

"Don't you think it would be better if we went today? Forget those arrangements—"

The words died on his tongue as she popped out of the walk-in to level him with a pointed stare. He shouldn't wake the beast.

Rio had taken to royal life like a duck to water in Bagumi. Her contract with Tempo had ended back in January, and she'd wanted them to return here afterwards. It had coincided with their official wedding. Her family indulged in all the Indian traditions. Rio and Zediah not doing the *saat phere* again but instead settling for the *saptapadi*, walking seven steps together instead of the seven rounds with the sacred fire.

His mother got the February event she had wanted all along, which had helped to soothe the rift they'd created with their elopement. Queen Sapphire had gotten the Valentine's Day wedding she had wished for, too.

She'd turned out to be their biggest champion. Ever since walking a distraught Rio back to her room that fateful day, she had sweetly whispered in the king's ear to give them a chance. She'd even learned the blessing an elder was supposed to provide a married Indian woman. To her, the king's reaction that night had been no surprise.

And speaking of the king, he had gifted them a centre for performing arts as a wedding gift. The building was still being erected, but it didn't mean Rio wasn't a busy bee.

Bagumians had fallen in love with her, with her simplicity, winsome smile, and the fact she spoke Creole. Granted, it was with a weird accent, but the mother tongue from Mauritius, where her mum was from, took her in good stead with the locals here who had adopted her into their fold. Her Royal Highness Princess Riona was in much demand for official outings now.

As for the noon departure, Rio always had them arrange flights involving Nour during the day. She wanted him to be able to turn in for the night at whatever destination they were heading to, so trips had to happen during the daytime. This particular jump would see them in London for the next two weeks.

It meant going to see his in-laws, and though he loved Rio's family, there was no love lost between him and his mother-in-law. The woman gave him the creeps, and he knew how much of a bigot she really was, though she behaved in their presence. Guess him coming with an HRH title and giving one to her daughter had soothed the sting of him being a Black man. Frankly, if he never saw her again, it would be no loss. It comforted him the same could be said for Rio, who didn't allow her mother to walk all over her. Nour also didn't seem impressed by the older woman.

But this trip had a whole other reason for being on their schedule. Humphrey had proposed to Martha a while back, soon after she'd taken over for Rio as the Executive Director of Tempo. Martha's strongest wish was for her husband to dance the waltz with her during their late spring wedding. Rio was going to teach two-left-feet Humphrey how to waltz without making a fool of himself on the dance floor.

But this pregnancy changed everything. She should be slowing down now, right? Exertion wouldn't be good for the baby.

"Popping out for a few." He tightened his hold on his son and exited the wing they had been given as their private apartments in the palace.

He made a game of hopping in a sprint for one

corridor, then stopping short at the crossroads. Nour found this hilarious. The baby was still laughing when they entered Zareb's office in the administrative wing of the main castle. Like him, his twin was also an early riser.

"Beb!" Nour screamed when seeing his uncle, then lurched in his direction.

Zediah letting go and Zareb catching the bundle had become a well-practised dance by this point. However, Zareb had still not perfected the art of sweeping his locs aside before the feral kid fell onto them to munch away.

Zediah left his brother to deal with taking the toy-of-the-moment from the boy and dropped onto a seat in front of the desk.

"What's up?" Zareb asked.

"Hush hush, just between us, Rio's pregnant." He smiled as he recalled they'd used this phrase among them, siblings, as kids when exchanging rumours or outright secrets.

"Congratulations, man!" A frown settled on the man's face. "What's the matter?"

Zediah sighed. "I need a guard with her at all time. Female, as she is not to lift a single finger, and someone should be able to go inside the loo with her if she needs her hair held back when vomiting or something."

"You know she will kill me if I make this happen. Then she'll round on you."

Defeated, he sagged in the seat. "Yeah. She shouldn't exert herself, though. And now, with all those talks from Dad to make her Special Advisor for Arts and Culture. Think I could get her to defer taking the position for another year? The baby would be born, and she would have recovered post-partum by then."

A snort came from Zareb. "Dream on!"

That was right, too. He groaned and brought his

hands up to his bald head. He'd tried the look once, and Rio had fallen hook, line, and sinker for it. No way could he ever grow his hair back again. Though, with the way things were going, he wouldn't have much hair left soon.

"Man, you are so totally pussy-whipped!"

He looked up at his twin and frowned. "Your turn will come."

Zareb cackled.

"I sincerely doubt it." A pause followed, then he continued. "Zed, a word of advice?"

He nodded in acknowledgement.

"Love her, trust her, yet have her back. Isn't that the essence of marriage?"

True enough. If his brother had understood this, relationships shouldn't scare him so much.

Getting up, he reached for his son and peeled the recalcitrant kid from the arms of Uncle Beb. As he made for the door, he stopped on the threshold and turned back to his twin.

"Trust me on this. Your time will come, too."

Exiting the office, he wished his brothers well. He hoped they all found the kind of love he shared with Rio and Nour. Although they might lose their hair to all the hoopla, it was worth it. Who needed hair, anyway, when they had their person?

Yes, he sincerely hoped for all his brothers to find their woman.

THE END

Thank you for reading **The Torn Prince by Zee Monodee**, Royal House of Saene Book 4. Please leave a review on the site of purchase.

ABOUT THE AUTHOR

Of Indian heritage & a 2x breast cancer survivor, Zee lives in paradise (aka Mauritius!) with her long-suffering husband, their smart-mouth teenage son, and their tabby cat who thinks herself a fearsome feline from the nearby African Serengeti plains. When she isn't in her kitchen rolling out chapattis or baking cakes while singing along to the latest pop hit topping the charts, she can be found reading or catching up on her numerous TV show addictions. In her day job, she is an editor who helps other authors like her hone their works and craft.

Website: http://www.zeemonodee.com/
Facebook: facebook.com/zee.monodee
Instagram: instagram.com/zeemonodee/

Keep reading for an excerpt from _The Resolute Prince by Nana Prah_, Royal House of Saene Book 5.

EXCERPT—The Resolute Prince by Nana Prah

Zareb bowed to Queen Zulekha of Bagumi.

Seated on a maroon and gold patterned loveseat in her chambers, she tilted her face for his kiss, which he obliged.

Stepping back, his gaze lingered on the person he'd initially assumed to be a female who shared the couch with his mother.

Delicate features of high cheekbones and a narrow-bridged nose in a slim face had deceived him. Closer inspection of the stranger who had stood and bowed revealed a flat chest, smooth skin with no hint of stubble, and closely shorn hair.

Their visitor was a young man—an effeminate-looking one, to be sure.

"Good evening," Zareb greeted.

"Dear heart, won't you have a seat," his mother said with a wave of her hand.

He struggled to maintain an indiscernible expression. It grated on his nerves when she called him anything but his given name, and she knew it. Years of attempting to divert his distaste at the endearment had failed.

"Thank you, Mama."

He chose an armchair across from the duo to best observe them.

His mother turned to the young man and touched his shoulder. "This is Maliq Sule Ahvanti. Everyone calls him Sule. Meet Prince Zareb Aamori Saene, my third child. Son of the King of Bagumi and head of security here at the palace."

Zareb's ears sharpened with interest at the pride in his mother's voice.

Sule's angled mahogany-brown eyes stayed on him.

Zareb felt a brush of heat at the back of his neck and raised his hand to rub it as his muscles stiffened in full alert.

"It's a pleasure to meet you, Your Highness." The voice came out with a minimal huskiness as if the young man hadn't yet gone through puberty. Perhaps he'd overestimated the boy's age.

Instead of responding in a like manner, Zareb tipped his head.

Of what relevance was being a prince if one didn't demonstrate arrogance every once in a while? Or rather, every day of his life.

Sule's mouth tightened into as straight a line as a person with such full lips could achieve. His gaze never wavered as Zareb studied those feminine features. The boy's insolence intrigued him.

A strong-willed individual.

Most people would be fidgeting or at least would have looked away at his concentrated perusal.

"Sule is the child of a close friend. A sister."

Zareb yielded to his mother's dissolution of the stare-off by shifting his gaze to the queen.

"We attended the same boarding school and had maintained our friendship ever since. Do you recall Eshe's visits here and us to her?"

"I do. You two giggled and gossiped the whole time you were together."

To his horror, his mother's eyes watered. She plucked a tissue from the box on the coffee table and dabbed the tears away before they could slide too far down her flawless cheeks.

"She was a wonderful woman."

His mother's grief when she'd heard of her friend's death had placed a pall of sorrow over the palace. Zawadi, Amira, their half-brother Zik, and his stepmother, Queen Sapphire, escorted her to the funeral. The crushing empathy Zareb had felt at his mother's grief had made it impossible for him to travel with the delegation.

Fingers clawed into a fist as he retrained from rubbing his chest at the lingering hurt on behalf of his mother's loss.

The grim smile she shared with Sule emphasized her heartbreak.

"Four months gone, and I miss her terribly."

Sule's smooth throat bobbed with his hard swallow. His eyes glistened before he bowed his head. "She spoke highly and often of you, Your Majesty."

The heft of sorrow lifted when the queen cleared her throat before clapping her hands once.

"My sweet son, my guest would like to be trained in fencing. It would give me immense pleasure if you were to guide him as his personal coach."

Now she was spreading it on a little too thick.

Rather than deny his mother's request outright, which would turn into a battle of wills, Zareb decided to encourage the young man to change his mind. "How old are you, boy."

His narrow, slumped shoulders straightened. "Eighteen."

Zareb scoffed. "What happened to your voice? You sound like a girl."

OTHER BOOKS BY LOVE AFRICA PRESS

Unravelling His Mark by Zee Monodee

Love on a Mission by Jomi Oyel

Fading Face by Jonah Igwe

The Tainted Prince by Kiru Taye

CONNECT WITH US

Facebook.com/LoveAfricaPress

Twitter.com/LoveAfricaPress

Instagram.com/LoveAfricaPress

www.loveafricapress.com

LOVE AFRICA
PRESS
African Love Stories

CPSIA information can be obtained
at www.ICGtesting.com
Printed in the USA
LVHW110425130821
695221LV00009B/1134